THE STONE & THE PANTRY

The Stone & The Pantry

SHAWN VIVEIROS

For Sophia,
Who helped me find the magic tucked behind an
old pantry door, and reminded me that the best
adventures begin with a little spark of imagination,
encouragement, and a lot of heart.

Contents

Chapter 1

The Journey to a New Life

It's a typical Tuesday—warm, sunny, and full of potential—except for one young girl. Eleanor Kravitz, eleven years old, sits in the backseat of her parents' car, as nervous as a cat in a thunderstorm. They're moving to Point Rock, a small town perched on the edge of the sprawling metropolis where she grew up.

Staring out the window, Eleanor anxiously pets her best friend and loyal companion, Charlie. The Australian Cattle Dog nudges his long black nose into her lap, sensing her unease and offering comfort the only way he knows how.

"Honey, you're doing it again," Eleanor's father said from the driver's seat, catching her in the rearview mirror. "You're petting Charlie so much there's hair all over the car."

"Sorry. I'm just... trying to keep him calm," Eleanor replied, her voice low, her fingers still moving through Charlie's fur.

Eleanor didn't look like someone who belonged in the middle of nowhere. Her messy dark brown curls frizzed stubbornly no matter how often she tied them back, and her oversized sweatshirt—faded purple and bearing the logo of her old city school—swallowed her petite frame. Her jeans had a hole in one knee—not from fashion, but from climbing the chain-link fence behind her old building. Her sneakers were scuffed, and one of her socks didn't match. She always looked like she was headed somewhere important, even if she wasn't sure where that was.

But it was her eyes that told the real story—sharp, observant, a little wary. The kind of eyes that noticed things others didn't. That cataloged details and connected dots. A thinker's eyes. A seeker's. Even now, those eyes didn't blink as the countryside blurred past her window. She was memorizing it. Just in case.

Her mother chimed in gently, "There's nothing to worry about. You're going to love this town. You'll be able to ride your bike everywhere—no traffic, no big crowds. I know you miss your old home and your friends, but this is a good move for your dad and me. You'll make new friends in no time. Really, there's nothing to worry about."

"Why couldn't we just stay where we were?" Eleanor asked, her tone slipping into a whine. "I liked it there. So did Charlie."

"I know, sweetheart," her father said, his tone softening. "But sometimes you have to go where the opportunities are. This one just... landed in our lap. You'll see. Give it time—you'll grow to love this place."

Her parents hadn't exactly planned on uprooting their lives. But when the letter arrived—crisp paper, odd seal, no return address—it changed everything. It turned out that an old house in a nearly forgotten town called Point Rock had fallen into their laps. Not through any will or distant cousin's generosity, but through a strange web of small-town paperwork and family history that no one fully understood. Something about Eleanor's grandfather, Levi Kravitz, being the last registered descendant of a church official who once lived there. Eleanor barely knew him. He was quiet, serious, more comfortable with old books and gardening gloves than conversation. He'd moved to the city as a teenager and rarely spoke of Point Rock, except to say it was "where things used to be simpler." He died a few years back, and none of this—none of this house business—had ever come up. Still, the paperwork checked out, and the house, while old and creaky and covered in ivy, was officially theirs.

And as if the universe were stacking the deal even higher, a job transfer followed. Both her mom and dad had worked for years at the largest Henry Brothers grocery store in the city—clocking long hours, climbing the ladder, doing everything right. Then suddenly, a position opened at the regional headquarters. A promotion. Better hours. Better pay. And it just so happened to be located in Point Rock, less than ten minutes from the inherited property. It was almost too perfect. Her parents called it a blessing. Eleanor called it suspicious.

To her, it didn't feel like fate. It felt like being plucked from everything she knew—her friends, her school, the corner store that still carried her favorite gum—and dropped into a town with no sidewalks, a single blinking stoplight, and a history she hadn't asked to be part of. Sure, the move made sense on paper. But to Eleanor, it was just a big question mark with a house from a man she barely knew in a town he left behind. That wasn't a blessing. That was baggage.

Eleanor stared out the rear window, watching trees whip past—one after another, a blur of green with no sign of houses or buildings. It felt endless, like they were driving away from everything familiar and into something forgotten. Her memories clung to the road behind them, trailing like mist in the car's wake.

As they neared the edge of town, the forest gave way to open stretches of land—wide, silent, and unsettling. Acre after acre of rotted leaves and dying plants sprawled out like a graveyard of failed crops. What might once have been farmland was now a barren patchwork of cracked soil and wilted trees, pale and brittle at the edges. The land looked haunted.

Then, almost suddenly, the emptiness broke. Small buildings began to pop up from the fields—white, yellow, and blue houses dotting the landscape like scattered marbles. A few looked modern, but most were worn with age. And one house, towering above the rest, stood out like something from a different world.

"Whoa, look at that house—it's huge!" Eleanor exclaimed, her interest sparking for the first time since they'd left the city.

"That must be Mr. Henry's place," her father replied. "I'd guess he's the wealthiest man in town. Started that whole chain of grocery stores right here. Your mother and I both work for the company—the main office is just a few miles from here."

"Is our house going to be this nice?" Eleanor asked, leaning forward between the seats with hope in her voice.

"Well, we're just about to turn into the town center," her mother said, a note of pride sneaking in. "You'll see it in a second—just around this corner!"

Eleanor had only ever known the city. Born there, raised there, she'd spent all eleven years of her life surrounded by the familiar buzz of buses, crowds, and concrete. Her idea of "the country" was mosquitoes and muddy fields. In the city, her days were full; school with hundreds of other kids, afternoons in the courtyard of their apartment building, evenings echoing with laughter. That was her normal.

But as the car rounded the corner, her excitement fizzled. There was no cozy home in sight. Just a few tired brick office buildings, a lonely little bank, a trailer-sized post office—and an old, vine-choked church sagging under its own weight.

As they pulled into the center of town, a strange chill crept into Eleanor's thoughts. This place wasn't just different—it felt... hollow. Haunted. Her fears solidified the moment she saw the moving truck parked beside the church.

This wasn't a detour. This was home.

"Is this... where we're going to live?" Eleanor asked, her voice tight with disbelief, a lump rising in her throat.

"Oh, it's not that bad," her father said, hoisting bags from the car. "I know it's old and not what you're used to, but it's got that country charm."

"We got a really good deal on it, sweetheart," her mother added, signing paperwork with the movers. "And I'm hoping you'll help us fix it up. Look at Charlie—he loves it here!"

Charlie, nose to the ground, was already exploring every crack and crevice of the yard. He weaved between weeds and porch steps, sniffing, marking, investigating—completely oblivious to Eleanor's horror. A free spirit through and through, Charlie thrived on trouble and discovery, happiest when he was chasing after something he probably shouldn't.

"Why don't you take Charlie for a walk and explore a little while we unpack?" her mother suggested, pointing toward the quiet, empty street. "Your bike's around back by the utility shed. Just be careful—there's hardly any traffic, but still..."

"C'mon, Charlie," Eleanor said with a sigh, clipping the leash to his collar. "Let's see what we can find in this... nothin' town," she mumbled.

They rounded the house, passing close to the overgrown lot next door where the old church sagged in the weeds. Eleanor stuck close to the strip of neatly mowed grass, keeping Charlie ahead of her—just in case something jumped out from the wild side.

"You'll protect me, won't you, Charlie?" she said, mostly to herself. Charlie's tail wagged in reply, his steps light and eager.

By the shed stood a massive metal container left by the movers, its doors still yawning open, hinges groaning with every breeze. The creaking made Eleanor flinch—just for a second—before she spotted her bike leaning nearby.

"Goose," she whispered with a smile.

The bold black letters spelled Mongoose, outlined in bright orange. Eleanor had named the bike after a neighborhood game back in the city—printed a sticker of a cartoon goose with aviator goggles and slapped it on her helmet. It made her feel like a fighter pilot, like someone brave.

"Ready. Set. Go!" she shouted, snapping the leash to a makeshift hook on the handlebars. "Goose flies once more!"

And just like that, she and Charlie were off—tearing through the tall grass, heading for the street.

Eleanor and Charlie zipped through the yard, flattening the tall grass on their way to the street. With a glance left, then right, they slipped onto the road like it belonged to them.

The town felt... empty. No cars. No pedestrians. Not even another kid on a bike. As Eleanor coasted past a row of tidy brick office buildings, she noticed how pristine everything was—no graffiti, no trash, not even a single broken window. Just silence and space.

Houses peeked out from behind thick trees, gravel driveways spaced like teeth in a sleepy smile. Every hundred feet, another one appeared—blue, white, yellow—small patches of life breaking up the woods.

At the end of the road, Eleanor stopped at a lonely stop sign. Across the street stretched a dull, dead field—what once might've been a farm, now looked like it had given up.

"Well, Charlie," she muttered, "I guess this is it. Our new home. Nothing but trees and tired old land." She kicked at a stone. "What else is there to see?"

With curiosity tugging at her handlebars, she turned in the opposite direction from where they'd arrived and followed a winding path through quiet neighborhoods. The streets bent around clusters of houses before spitting her out near a more active part of town—if you could call it that.

Here stood the largest building she'd seen so far; a brick structure that held the town hall, library, and school—all in one. One building. One school. For every kid in town. Nothing like the city.

She circled it slowly, eyeing the soccer field and the fenced-in baseball diamond. She stopped at a fountain by the gate, filled her bottle, and squirted a stream of water toward Charlie, who tried to snap at it mid-air.

"Tomorrow," she whispered, staring at the school, "I'll be walking in through those doors."

Eleanor wasn't usually shy, but something about this place made her chest feel tight. As she walked her bike home, her footsteps grew heavier, her confidence softer. She had no friends here. No familiarity. Just empty buildings and too much quiet.

"I don't know, Charlie," she said, her shoulders slumping. "What do you think of this town?"

Charlie didn't answer, of course—just trotted ahead, tail wagging like he hadn't noticed the silence at all.

Dusk had settled by the time Eleanor and Charlie returned. The windows of their new house glowed with warm light—her mother unpacking in the kitchen, her father on the porch sweeping cobwebs off the beams. Eleanor approached slowly, dragging her feet, still half-hoping it was a dream.

Charlie had other plans.

"Charlie! Wait—slow down!" she called as he suddenly lunged toward the house, leash taut in her hands.

The leash slipped from her fingers and hit the pavement. She scrambled to regain control but nearly toppled over her bike. In one smooth motion, she swung back onto the seat, gritted her teeth, and pedaled hard—chasing her runaway dog with every ounce of determination she had left.

Charlie ran like a rocket, leash whipping in the air behind him. Eleanor leaned forward, peddling faster, lungs burning. She caught up just as her front tire hit the grass. She skidded to a stop at the foot of the porch.

"Welcome home!" her father said with a crooked smile. "Did you see a monster or something?"

"N-no, just racing... Charlie," Eleanor panted, doubled over the handlebars. "There's nothing to do in this town," she muttered, trudging up the porch steps.

She glanced around—her dad had already swept most of the porch clean, stacking debris in a tidy pile. With a heavy sigh, she dropped onto the porch swing, elbows on knees, chin in hands. Her father joined her a moment later.

"I know this is hard," he said gently, placing a hand on her shoulder. "But this is a good opportunity for us. With a little paint and elbow grease, it won't be so bad."

Eleanor didn't reply. She just closed her eyes.

And then—snap.

Her arms shot upward as the swing gave out beneath her. Rusted chains snapped with a sharp twang, and she and her father crashed to the floor in a heap.

"Ouch! I hate this place already!" Eleanor groaned, sprawled in a cloud of dust.

"Guess we need more than just paint, huh?" her dad said, coughing through a laugh.

The screen door banged open. "Is everyone okay?" her mother called, rushing out.

"We're fine. Just... a little home improvement project," her father said, brushing dust off his shirt.

Eleanor sat up, cheeks flushed, arms and face streaked with sweat and grime. She looked from one parent to the other and then down at herself. Sticky, dusty, and disgusted.

"Eleanor, go grab a snack, take a shower, and get ready for bed," her mom said softly, guiding her toward the door. "Tomorrow's a big day."

Eleanor stared at the house. At the peeling paint and broken porch. Everyone seemed so happy. Even Charlie. But she wasn't. And tomorrow, she had to start a brand new school.

Chapter 2

A Dark Secret
Emerges

The alarm clock buzzed like a mosquito in Eleanor's ear—loud, sharp, and completely unforgiving. She fumbled across the nightstand, smacking around for the snooze button until, finally, silence.

Sitting up with a groan, she blinked at the mess of boxes and strange shadows around her. For a moment, she forgot where she was. Then it hit her; today was the first day at her new school.

"Ugh," she muttered, throwing off the blanket and stumbling toward a half-open box. Clothes were crammed everywhere. She dug like a dog in a sandbox until she found a wrinkled T-shirt and a pair of jeans near the bottom of a box shoved into the closet.

Eleanor didn't care much for fashion or whatever outfits were trending on her classmates' social feeds. She preferred clothes she could move in—things that wouldn't tear if she climbed a tree, skidded her bike through gravel, or dove for a soccer ball. Comfort always beat style, especially when adventure could strike at any moment.

"Eleanor?" her mom's voice called through the door. "Are you almost ready? I can drop you off today."

"Almost! Just looking for my backpack!" she called back, already glancing around the floor.

"Try the living room boxes," her mom suggested. "And remember—you've got less than fifteen minutes! Your dad and I will finish unpacking while you're at school."

Eleanor rolled her eyes and sighed, then opened the door. "I'm ready now," she announced.

Her mom took one whiff and recoiled, fanning the air. "Not with that breath, you're not. Ew. Brush your teeth and meet me in the car. Ten minutes!"

Eleanor brushed her teeth, found her backpack, stuffed a granola bar in her pocket, and shuffled out to the car. She slumped into the passenger seat, her stomach fluttering like a leaf caught in wind. Her fingers picked at the hem of her sleeve, a nervous habit she hadn't outgrown since third grade. She wondered if the other kids would notice her worn-out sneakers or if they'd care that her backpack still had a keychain from her old school's science fair. She didn't want to stand out—but she didn't want to disappear, either. Before she could dwell on any of it too long, the ride was over—and she was walking through the steel-and-glass front doors of her new school, the building swallowing her up before she had time to change her mind.

The entryway was quiet. A wide open space with dull tile floors and hallways stretching to the left and right. Eleanor paused on the school's painted logo in the center of the lobby—a stylized bird of prey in swooping flight, its wings outstretched and talons curled mid-clutch. Painted in bold blue and orange, it looked fierce in a generic, try-hard way, like every other middle school mascot trying to prove it was tougher than it really was. Eleanor stared at it for a moment, then spun slowly in place, scanning for any sign of where to go next.

"Eleanor?"

The voice came from the hallway to the left. A boy with shaggy brown hair and oversized glasses stepped into view, holding a clipboard like it was an extension of his arm. "Hi! I'm Oliver. Class president. It's my official duty to welcome you to our school—and give you a tour!" he added, beaming with pride.

"Uh... hi," Eleanor replied, blinking in confusion.

Oliver looked like he had been waiting his whole life for this moment. His shaggy brown hair flopped slightly over one eye, and thick glasses magnified his already-wide eyes just enough to make him look constantly surprised. He wore a button-down shirt tucked into cargo pants that didn't quite match, and his sneakers squeaked with every other step. A pen was clipped to his collar like a badge of honor, and his lanyard read STUDENT COUNCIL in bold block letters. He didn't seem nervous—just... earnest. Too earnest, maybe. Like someone who practiced being friendly in the mirror every morning.

"Come on," Oliver said, already motioning her down the hallway. "The layout's pretty simple. The building's basically one big rectangle—two main hallways that run front to back, and classrooms along the sides."

As they walked, Eleanor glanced at the lockers between the classroom doors—about a dozen in each row, alternating blue and orange. It gave the otherwise beige-and-white walls a pop of color. She peeked into one of the classrooms. Ten desks. Maybe twelve. A huge difference from the city, where students were packed into rooms like sardines in a can.

"Library and cafeteria are just over here in the center of the building," Oliver said, pointing as they passed a set of wide glass doors. "Gym's through those double doors, and bathrooms are at the end of each hallway, on both sides. Pretty easy to remember."

Eleanor said nothing. Backpack slung over one shoulder, she stood there blinking, trying to take it all in. Her thoughts crept in like fog—memories of her old school, her friends, the noise and comfort of the city. This place felt empty. Too quiet. Too neat. A shiver traced her spine.

"Hey, are you okay?" Oliver asked, his voice softer now.

"Yeah, I'm fine. Where's my classroom?" she asked, sharper than she meant to.

"Right here—it's 126. Same as mine, actually. I'll walk you over. There's not much else to see."

They looped back down the hallway, past the cafeteria, where the unmistakable smell of overly steamed vegetables and tray food wafted into the corridor. The first bell rang overhead, sending students out of the shadows and into motion.

Eleanor's stomach tightened. Flashbacks from her old school flooded in—laughter, familiar faces, loud hallways. And now... this. New everything.

Oliver stopped in front of a beige door with a brass plaque: Room 126.

"Here you go," he said, backing away with an awkward grin. "Let me know if you need anything else. Class President's honor."

Eleanor took a deep breath, filling her lungs, then slowly let it out through her nose. Her fingers hovered on the doorknob as she thought to herself, "Just open it. It's just a classroom."

She turned the knob. The door creaked open. A dozen heads swiveled. Every eye landed on her.

Eleanor froze. For a split second, she imagined herself as some strange specimen under glass—like an alien dropped in from a far-off planet. Her heart thumped like a drum.

"You must be Eleanor," said the teacher, motioning her inside. "Welcome. I'm Mrs. Newman. You can take that open seat there—we were just getting started."

Eleanor walked stiffly to the empty desk, each step heavier than the last. She could feel the stares crawling across her backpack, her sneakers, her clothes. But as she sat, the tension shifted. Most of the students were already back to their notes or whispering to friends. A few barely noticed her at all.

She let out the breath she didn't realize she'd been holding.

"Okay, class," Mrs. Newman said, her voice bright but firm. "Today we're going to learn about the first nations that lived in this region."

Eleanor sat up straighter. "First nations?" She muttered to herself.

"I know most of you already know the legend of the Giving Basket," Mrs. Newman continued. "But let's get Eleanor up to speed. Can I get a few volunteers to write some facts on the board?"

Three students stood, grabbed markers, and began scribbling on the whiteboard. Eleanor watched as the facts appeared, one by one:

- **The native tribe helped settlers survive the harsh climate.**

- A special ceremony produced an abundance of food.
- The Giving Basket was not an actual basket—but a sacred place.

Mrs. Newman nodded. "Great job. We'll dig deeper into the real history, but those are some of the main points. Eleanor, we'll have books in the library if you want to catch up on the legend in more detail."

Eleanor scribbled notes like her life depended on it. She didn't like falling behind—never had—and this new school, with its unfamiliar faces and echoing hallways, already made her feel two steps behind everyone else. Taking good notes was her way of anchoring herself, a quiet rebellion against the chaos. If she couldn't control where she lived or what school she went to, at least she could control this. Her handwriting, neat but quick, filled the margins of the page with bullet points and side comments, arrows looping to underlined phrases. She boxed important facts and starred anything that sounded like it might be on a quiz. The pencil wore down fast, the tip grinding flatter with each pass, but she didn't stop—not even when her hand started to cramp. Her stomach gave a quiet growl, but she barely noticed. She was focused, locked in, clinging to the comfort of order in a world that had rearranged itself overnight.

The bell for lunch rang like a lifeline.

She packed her things and followed the flow of students to the cafeteria, but the smell hit her before she even stepped inside—industrial food trays, mashed potatoes, corn, something brown that may or may not have been meat, and of course... chicken nuggets. They were everywhere.

Her appetite dropped like a stone.

Grabbing an apple from the fruit tray, she scanned the room for an open seat—but the thought of sitting down with total strangers sent a cold wave through her. Without hesitation, she veered toward the glowing red EXIT sign by the cafeteria doors. Just beyond it, the library, her old safe haven back home.

Eleanor slipped inside. The doors closed behind her with a soft whoosh, muting the noise of lunchroom chaos.

The library was quiet. Dusty. Comforting. It smelled like paper and wood polish. She relaxed slightly and headed for a table near the courtyard window, but before she could reach it—

"Excuse me, dear. Are you the new student?" The voice came from a corner desk. An elderly woman with soft gray hair and tiny glasses perched at the tip of her nose looked up from a stack of books.

"I don't recognize you?" the woman repeated softly. "You must be the new transfer we talked about at staff meeting this morning."

Eleanor turned toward the voice. The librarian had kind eyes, creased at the corners, and lips pursed like she was holding back a thousand secrets. Thin glasses rested on the tip of her nose, glinting in the library's muted light.

Eleanor nodded.

The woman tilted her head. "Did your family move into the old church rectory?"

"Yeah," Eleanor replied. "Just yesterday."

"Hmm," the librarian murmured. "What a tragedy that was."

Eleanor's eyebrows lifted. "What do you mean... tragedy?"

The librarian blinked, as if surprised by her own words. "Oh—just old stories. Town tales. Nothing to worry about," she said too quickly. "Now, what can I help you find today, dear?"

Eleanor narrowed her eyes just slightly. She knew that tone—when an adult brushed something off too fast. It always meant there was something more to it.

"Actually," Eleanor said, switching into her best model-student voice, "Mrs. Newman wanted me to learn about the town's history, so I can catch up with the class. Where can I find the history section?"

"Ah! Excellent," the librarian said, rising from her chair with surprising energy. "Right this way."

She led Eleanor to a quiet alcove tucked in the back corner. Shelves lined the wall—black boxes with years printed in faded white labels. Below them sat an odd-looking machine. A monitor, knobs, and something that looked like a film reel.

"These are the old newspaper archives," the librarian explained. "You'll find County Press records here, and town documents. This is a microfilm reader—it'll help you view the old articles. Instructions are posted there," she said, pointing to a laminated sheet tacked to the wall.

She gestured to another set of shelves. "These books are mostly local history. Some are about the town itself, others about native traditions. Let me know if you need anything else, dear."

Eleanor stood alone in the alcove, the hum of the microfilm machine filling the silence. She looked over the black boxes of old records, each one holding pieces of stories long forgotten.

What kind of tragedy gets buried in a town like this? she wondered.

With a flick of determination, she pulled down the first box and got to work.

Eleanor sat down in front of the glowing screen and typed in her first search; 'Church' and 'Rectory'.

Hundreds of results.

Her heart sank a little. There were too many articles to go through. She needed something stronger. Something sharper.

She added one more word; 'Murder'.

The list shrank. Now, just two articles.

One from August 1968. The other from January 1969.

Eleanor clicked the first. The headline snapped into view:

PASTOR OF 41 YEARS MURDERED IN HOME

Her eyes flew across the page. She followed the instructions from the laminated sheet—scroll, zoom, adjust the contrast. The text flickered in front of her.

The victim, Reverend Thomas Holland, was found in the early hours of August 14th. The long-time pastor was believed to have been attacked in his own home—the rectory attached to the historic church. No arrests were made. Local authorities suspect the involvement of drifters, often sheltered by the church's charity program...

Eleanor's mouth went dry.

That's our house.

She pushed back from the screen for a second, stunned. Then leaned back in.

In memory of Reverend Holland, a new church will be built with funds donated by the Henry Brothers Grocery Chain.

Her eyebrows lifted. Henry again.

Eleanor loaded the second article.

OLD CHURCH TO REMAIN UNDER CARE OF PARISHIONERS

She skimmed. Most of it talked about ownership rights and building transfers, until one name stopped her cold.

'Levi Kravitz'.

The property rights were granted to the church secretary, Sister Elizabeth Matthews, and altar boy Levi Kravitz, named as beneficiaries in Reverend Holland's will...

Another line jumped out; *The rectory and attached church may only be owned by direct descendants of the two listed beneficiaries. It may not be sold or transferred to outside parties—specifically, the Henry family.*

Eleanor's heart pounded.

That wasn't just a weird story or a town legend. This was personal.

Eleanor stared at the screen, rereading the line; *'The rectory and church may only be owned by descendants of Sister Elizabeth Matthews and altar boy Levi Kravitz...'*

Her hands trembled slightly on the edge of the desk.

That was her grandfather.

And someone, specifically the Henry family; wasn't allowed to own the property.

This wasn't just folklore. This wasn't just a spooky house. It was history. Her family history now.

The school bell rang overhead, sharp and sudden, breaking the spell.

Eleanor blinked. She quickly rewound the film, placed the box back on the shelf, and gathered her things. Her mind buzzed louder than the machine.

As she passed the librarian on her way out, she paused just long enough to deliver a parting shot.

"Thanks for your help," she said, then smiled. "Oh—and my name's Eleanor. Eleanor Kravitz."

The librarian's expression froze. Her eyes widened. She stared at Eleanor like she'd just seen a ghost—or a prophecy fulfilled.

Eleanor didn't wait for a reply. She slipped out the library doors, a grin still tugging at the corner of her mouth.

She couldn't wait for school to end.

Something was happening here. And she was going to find out exactly what.

Chapter 3

Searching for the Unusual

The final bell rang like freedom. Eleanor bolted from her seat and raced to the bus, dodging backpacks and slow walkers like she was escaping a crumbling temple in one of her favorite adventure movies. She made it out the front doors just in time to see the buses rumbling into place, each one groaning like a metal beast reluctantly doing its job.

Bus seating wasn't assigned, but everyone knew the rules. The back of the bus was sacred ground—claimed by the cool kids, the loud kids, the ones who always had gum and earbuds and rumors to whisper. The front was a different story. That's where the rule-followers lived; kids who wore their ID lanyards outside of school, kids who told the teacher when someone was out of dress code, kids who brought carrot sticks in little zip-lock bags and made spreadsheets for fun. Sometimes the very front row housed the truly unfortunate—snack-pack thieves, known tattletales, or the poor souls who still needed assigned aides.

Eleanor aimed for the middle. The unspoken safe zone. Not cool enough to be noticed, not strange enough to be targeted. The middle was where kids disappeared between stops and no one ever remembered who sat there. And that was fine by her. After a day of new teachers, awkward stares, and invisible trip wires of social rules she hadn't learned yet, she didn't want to be seen—she just wanted to breathe.

She slipped into her seat, set her backpack beside her like a shield, and pressed her cheek to the cool window. The engine rumbled beneath her feet. The noise of the bus rose like a tide behind her, but in her quiet spot in the middle, it all faded into something soft and manageable. Her breath fogged the plastic window as she stared out at the blurred trees and sidewalks. Her brain was spinning, still stuck on the name; Levi Kravitz.

The bus rolled past the last few shops of downtown. Ahead, the old church loomed into view.

Eleanor sat up, grabbed her bag, and made her way to the front.

"Kravitz?" the driver said, scanning her route sheet.

"Yeah." Eleanor nodded, stepping down to the sidewalk.

"Wait!" the driver called after her. "Are you related to Levi Kravitz?"

Eleanor froze.

Slowly, she turned and met the driver's gaze. "Sounds familiar," she said with a shrug, trying to sound casual, but her heart was pounding.

She waved a quick goodbye and turned toward the house. Behind her, the bus doors folded shut, the driver still staring through the window like she was trying to solve a puzzle Eleanor hadn't given her all the pieces for.

As the bus engine rumbled and pulled away, Eleanor took a deep breath. Her stomach grumbled—a reminder that beneath all the mystery and nerves, she was still just a kid who hadn't eaten lunch.

The house stood there like it always did; crooked porch, broken swing, chipped paint. Somehow, it already felt more familiar than the school.

She stepped inside, and instantly—

Click-click-click-click!

Charlie's paws skittered across the hardwood. His bark echoed through the hallway as he launched himself toward her like a rocket made of fur.

"Hi, Charlie!" Eleanor said, her voice rising half an octave with joy. "I missed you too—and I'm starving. Let's find something to eat."

Charlie spun in a tight circle, tail wagging like a metronome on fast forward. Eleanor dropped her backpack near the door and made her way toward the kitchen, passing under the creaky banister, stepping around the same boxes, and hopping over the same rolled-up rug that hadn't moved an inch.

Like most old houses, the kitchen showed its age—and not in a charming, cozy way. The newer appliances stuck out like awkward guests at a vintage party. The pale sea-green cabinets sagged on their hinges, never fully shutting, while the countertop looked like white quartz trapped under a plastic shield from a time before fashion existed. A diamond-patterned brass backsplash—faded and a little warped—ran along the wall, clashing with peeling floral wallpaper that had once been cream, maybe. By the pantry door, a small worn wooden shelf stood in front of the wallpaper, now curled up at the edges, like it had given up holding on long ago.

Eleanor opened the pantry door.

Disappointment greeted her like an empty echo.

A few cans of beans. Chickpeas. Corn. A bag of potatoes slouched on the bottom shelf. Bread, rice, cereal—dry, beige, uninspired. Her parents clearly hadn't gone shopping yet. Judging by the coffee pot on the counter, they'd had enough energy to make caffeine, and at least milk... and that was about it.

She grabbed a yellow box of honey-oat cereal and turned toward the dining room, hopping over the rolled-up rug. She found the box labeled Plates/Bowls, fished out a plain white bowl, and leapt back over the rug like she'd done it a hundred times.

Spoon in hand, milk in bowl, she leaned over the counter and began eating—one spoonful at a time, slurping slowly as her thoughts churned.

This house is old. Really old. And weird.

With each bite, a new theory bubbled up; hidden staircases, secret doors, passageways behind bookshelves.

Maybe—just maybe—there was more to this house than creaky floors and bad wallpaper.

Eleanor wiped a streak of milk from her chin and reached into her backpack, pulling out the apple she'd stashed at lunch. With a loud crunch, she bit into it, eyes drifting toward Charlie.

He sat at the edge of the rug, head tilted, watching her like he was waiting for the next big adventure.

"Let's go explore the house," she said through a mouthful of apple. "There's gotta be more to it than this dusty old kitchen."

At the sound of her voice, Charlie jumped up with a happy bark and bounced in place, tail wagging like mad.

Mulling over where to start, Eleanor thought about all the old movies and mystery novels she loved—the ones with fabled haunted mansions, creaky hallways, and endless secrets tucked behind velvet drapes or loose bricks.

Secret passage behind a bookcase? A candlestick on the mantle that opens a hidden door? A tunnel in the basement leading to a lab or vault?

All possibilities. Some more terrifying than others.

Right next to the pantry sat the basement door. If a house like this was hiding something, that would be a prime suspect.

Eleanor turned the knob and opened the door.

Darkness.

She flicked the light switch up. Nothing. Then down and back up again. Still nothing. The black void at the bottom of the stairs stared back.

Charlie padded beside her and peered down the stairwell, nose twitching as the scent of must and mildew drifted up from below. He didn't move.

"Charlie, you first," Eleanor whispered.

Charlie stayed put.

Eleanor took a breath, then slowly stepped back and closed the door.

"We'll wait for Dad on this one, Charlie," she muttered. "I'm not ready to deal with any vampires, ghosts, or... whatever could be down there." She gave a short laugh—half-joking, half-nervous.

"C'mon, let's start upstairs."

They crossed the dining room, again hopping over the same rolled-up rug and weaving through the maze of unpacked boxes. At the base of the stairs, they passed the large living room on the other side of the hall—quiet and untouched.

Each step up the staircase came with a chorus of creaks and groans. The old wood bent, flexed, and protested under their weight.

At the top, Eleanor paused. Her room was to the right. The bathroom straight ahead. Two more bedrooms flanked either side of the hallway.

She chose the empty bedroom first.

It was plain—vaulted ceilings, faded wallpaper, and that eerie stillness that only empty rooms seem to hold. The only feature of note was a bump-out in the wall where the chimney passed through. No trap doors. No crawl spaces. No secret panels.

One by one, she and Charlie moved through the rooms. Each one the same; boring, empty, slightly spooky in a way that made her skin prickle—but no hidden staircases, no dusty attics tucked behind a hatch. The vaulted ceilings ruled that out.

The bathroom at the end of the hall had only one interesting feature; an old, freestanding iron tub—deep, heavy, and slightly off-kilter. A thin stream of water leaked at the floor drain, creating a slow, steady drip that had begun to stain the ceiling below in the dining room.

Eleanor stared at it for a moment, watching the droplets gather at the base. A mystery of the plumbing kind, she thought. Still creepy.

No trapdoors. No secret levers. No hidden tunnels.

Just a weird old house... and a growing feeling that it wasn't finished revealing itself.

"Charlie, I don't think we're going to find anything up here. Mom and Dad's room is just another plain square, like mine," Eleanor muttered as she headed back downstairs, the old wood groaning and squeaking beneath her feet once again.

Back on the main floor, she turned toward the living room—the large space on the other side of the staircase. It was bigger than she remembered from the walk-through, but colder, too. The kind of room that still carried someone else's air. Furniture stood like forgotten statues, half-wrapped in gray moving blankets, their shapes vaguely human in the right light. Boxes were stacked in the corners like fort walls, unopened and ominous, labeled in black marker with scrawled guesses—"Kitchen?", "Dad's tools", "Books?", as if even her parents weren't sure where anything belonged yet. An old floor lamp tilted near the window, missing its shade. It cast no light.

At one end stood a fireplace framed in heavy brick, dark with soot. Its iron grate was rusted and stubborn, and a heavy stone mantel jutted out just high enough to crack a skull if someone tripped. On either side, two towering bookshelves loomed—built into the wall, their upper shelves nearly touching the ceiling. Dust curled in the corners like spiderwebs just waiting to return. Eleanor stepped closer, brushing her fingers along the edge of one shelf, letting the fine powder coat her skin. These books hadn't been touched in a long time.

Most of the volumes were unfamiliar—stiff, gold-edged hardcovers bound in cracked leather and cloth, their spines labeled with titles like *Collected Histories of the New England Valley* and *The Eastern Almanac*. Some were grouped in matching sets, arranged by color rather than topic; deep navy blues, burnt oranges, forest greens. The kind of books that looked impressive but rarely got opened.

Near the bottom shelf sat a fading stack of old *National Geographic* magazines, their yellow spines lined up like a parade of tired sentries. They leaned against a row of smaller, more personal books; a well-worn Bible with curling corners, a Tolkien classic with a broken spine and brittle pages, and then... a slim, black leather notebook. It sat slightly askew, not tucked in like the others, but resting like it had been set down in a hurry. Waiting. Watching.

Eleanor reached toward it, her fingers hovering just above the cover, heart ticking just a little faster. Something about it felt... off. Not bad, exactly. Just... important.

"Hmm... this looks interesting," Eleanor said, crouching to get a better look.

She picked up the notebook. The leather was cracked and dry, rough to the touch. Once soft and elegant, it had aged into something weathered—like the rest of the house. Forgotten, lost, and unloved.

She opened it carefully.

Inside were scribbles, notes, fragments of thoughts—written in a hurried hand. At the top corner of the inside cover, one name was written in faded ink.

"Sister Elizabeth," Eleanor whispered, barely audible—even to herself.

The first page looked like a list of names—each one followed by a date and a time. Eleanor scanned down the entries until she reached the last line.

September, 1981 — 2:00 PM.

She paused, thinking. It had been decades ago. Whatever happened at that time... it had been the last.

Flipping the page, she found a mess of scribbles crowding the margins. Notes written in rushed, looping cursive that was nearly impossible to decipher.

On the next page, something clearer caught her eye; a house checklist, written in large, deliberate handwriting.

     ○   ~~Paint~~, ~~Nails~~, ~~Lumber~~, ~~Rug~~, ~~Door~~

Each item had been neatly crossed out.

On the back of that page was a strange roundish sketch—more like a loose spiral or swirling shape than anything specific. Opposite it, on the facing page, was what appeared to be an unfinished letter.

Eleanor read aloud, slipping into her best impression of an old, proper-sounding nun:

"To the Town Clerk,

I am writing to inform you that I have been placed in a new monastery outside of the state. I need to leave by the end of the year. Per the arrangement with Pastor Holland and the town, I expect the Town to uphold the agreement. Included in this letter is a list of names and addresses of the former parishioners. This is of the utmost importance for the protection of the sto—"

Eleanor blinked.

"The sto... what?" she whispered.

The sentence trailed off, abruptly cut. The next two pages had been torn out, the ragged edges still visible.

The rest of the notebook was blank.

She sat back, heart thudding.

A list of names. A town agreement. A missing letter. And a word cut short.

"Hmm," Eleanor muttered, staring at the page. "What could this be? Sto...? St'o..."

She mouthed the word slowly, trying to finish Sister Elizabeth's thought.

"Stove? Stoop? Story? It could be anything!"

She started pacing. "Stork? Store? Stock?"

A loud thump echoed from the kitchen.

Eleanor jumped, her grip tightening around the black leather notebook. The sudden sound jolted her from her spiraling thoughts, but only barely. Her mind was still tangled in the mystery of the missing word, her lips moving unconsciously as she whispered to herself.

"Storyboard?" she muttered, turning the corner. "No, no... Stoic? Stonemill? Stonecrop? What is it?"

She rounded the staircase in a half-daze, eyes unfocused, still flipping through the possibilities in her mind. Her thumb absentmindedly traced the edge of a torn page in the notebook as her feet carried her forward, guided more by habit than attention.

"Stool...? Ston—Sto—OOH!"

Her toe caught the rolled-up rug; the same rug she'd effortlessly hopped over at least three times that day, but this time, her stride was lazy, her balance off, and she hit it full-force. The notebook flew from her hand, and in a tangle of limbs and flannel, she tumbled to the floor with a hard thud, skidding a few inches across the dusty wood.

For a second, she just lay there, winded, stunned. "OW," she groaned, eyes squeezing shut as she rolled onto her back and glared at the ceiling. "I hate this house."

Her ponytail had come undone, and a strand of hair stuck to her cheek. She brushed it away angrily, then sat up with a grunt, rubbing her elbow where it had smacked the floor. As she gathered herself, she noticed the notebook lying a few feet away, open to the last full page—its delicate, looping handwriting almost taunting her. The sentence still ended abruptly at sto—

"I was getting to you," she muttered to the journal, crawling over to retrieve it. "Thanks for the trip."

That's when she saw it. The pantry door.

It was open. Just slightly. A narrow slice of shadow cracked between the frame and the wall—barely enough to notice before, but unmistakable now. Eleanor froze.

From the dark beyond the door came a sound—faint at first, then unmistakable, Snuffling. Licking. Slurping.

Eleanor's eyes narrowed. "Charlie..." she said in a low, accusatory whisper, slowly rising to her feet. "You better not be eating a mouse or something, ew!"

She crept toward the pantry like she was approaching a crime scene, one hand still clutching the journal, the other ready to grab Charlie's collar.

She threw open the door.

There he was—nose buried in the shadows of the bottom shelf, tail wagging, licking something she couldn't quite see.

"Charlie!" Eleanor yelled, reaching in to grab his collar.

But it was too late. Whatever he'd found—he'd already eaten it.

Eleanor looked around the pantry. The food on the shelves was untouched. Still sealed. Still bland. Nothing out of place. "So... what had Charlie eaten?"

Chapter 4

Charlie Conjures up an Appetite

Eleanor stood frozen as Charlie attempted to sneak past her into the kitchen, bobbing and weaving, trying to squeeze between her legs like a furry little fugitive. Determined to figure out what he'd eaten, she quickly closed the pantry door, trapping the suspect inside with her.

"You're not leaving the crime scene, Charlie. I caught you red-handed—or better yet, red-snouted!" she said while giggling.

Turning back to the shelves, Eleanor began mentally taking inventory.

A bag of flour. Brownie mix. Mac and cheese. Pistachios. Rice. A few boxes of pasta. Beans. Canned sweet corn. Canned peaches. A loaf of bread. Cake mix. Various spices.

To her amazement—or maybe just her poor memory—everything appeared to be there. Unmoved. Untouched. Uneaten.

She stepped back, only to stumble slightly on Charlie's wagging tail. Catching herself on the nearby coat rack, she heard the familiar sniffing and slurping again—right behind her.

Whipping around, Eleanor split the row of hanging coats like a curtain, pushing aside nylon, leather, and wool in dramatic fashion.

"A-HA!" Eleanor yelled, catching Charlie in the act once more. "Charlie, stop!"

She reached for his blue collar, the one with the little black paw prints. "Let me see what you've got there..."

Pulling him back gently, she revealed a reddish-brown bone—one of his favorites from back home.

A puzzled look crossed her face.

"Ew," she muttered. "Where did you find this? It looks like the bone I gave you last Christmas—but that was back at our old house. Like, a hundred miles away."

She hesitated, then shrugged. "Well, I guess you can have it. I thought you were chewing on some gross rat or something."

Letting go of his collar, Charlie dove back down, gnawing and slurping with noisy satisfaction, his eyes fluttering half-shut in bliss.

Eleanor slumped beside him with a sigh, giving him a gentle pat of praise—though her own stomach had other ideas.

Grrrrrumble.

"Charlie, now you've got me hungry again," she muttered. "I'd love to have what you're having... but not a bone. A big, juicy steak."

Her eyes drifted shut as the craving took over. "I can picture it now..." she murmured. "A sizzling bone-in rib-eye, thick and seared just right. A mountain of mashed potatoes, gravy spilling down like a river, crashing into a golden pile of buttery sweet corn."

She inhaled deeply. "I can smell it—like it's right in front of me. I can hear the sizzle—"

Her eyes flew open.

And there it was. A full dinner plate, exactly as she imagined—steak, potatoes, corn—fresh, hot, and steaming on the pantry floor.

Charlie was already up, bone abandoned, sprinting toward the miracle meal.

"Oh my—Charlie!" Eleanor gasped, jolting back against the wall. "How... what... ahhhh?!"

Words tumbled out in pieces as she scrambled to grab his collar.

Holding him back, heart pounding, she stared at the plate in stunned silence.

It was real. Exactly as she had imagined it.

"How—or where—did this come from?" Eleanor whispered, inching closer. She reached out with her pointer finger and gave the mashed potatoes a quick poke.

"Ahhhoooowwwwcccchhh!" she yelped, yanking her hand back. "It's really hot!"

She flicked the steaming potatoes from her fingertip, and the blob landed on the floor—right in front of Charlie.

Naturally, he lunged forward and licked it up.

"Charlie! No!" Eleanor cried, grabbing his collar—but it was too late. The mashed potatoes were gone.

She sat there, stunned. This couldn't be real.

Could it?

She could smell the food. Feel the heat. Hear the sizzle. And now... Charlie had eaten part of it.

This is real, she thought. This actually happened.

Kneeling forward, she crawled closer to the plate until she was just inches away. The steak looked perfectly seared. The mashed potatoes fluffed like clouds. The corn glistened with melted butter.

She turned to Charlie.

His eyes were locked on the plate—wide, fixated, hungry. The bone might as well not exist.

"Sorry, Charlie," she said with a grin, "but this one's mine."

She lifted the plate and sat upright, holding it carefully in her lap. The smell made her mouth water.

"Maybe I hit my head when I fell," she muttered. "Maybe this is all a dream. This is unreal…"

Just as she began to steady the plate, a familiar gnawing and slurping sound interrupted her thoughts.

She lowered the plate to see what Charlie was doing—and nearly dropped it right into her lap.

Beneath his head was another plate.

A white plate.

Just like hers.

Balancing the food in one hand, Eleanor reached out and snatched it.

"What! Wow! Charlie, how did you do that?!" Eleanor shouted, placing the half-eaten plate of steak, mashed potatoes, and corn back on the ground. "This looks like the same plate—the same food—even the same layout as mine!"

She stared in confusion and wonder as Charlie devoured his plate, tongue lashing at every last bit.

The thought struck her again—Maybe this really is a dream.

She looked down at the now slightly cooled food in her own hands. With a shrug, she stuck her finger into the warm, thick mashed potatoes, carefully scooping as much as she could balance on one finger. Raising her hand like a toast toward Charlie, she smiled.

"Cheers."

Then she popped the bite into her mouth.

"Wow," she gasped. "These are the best mashed potatoes I've ever had!"

Charlie didn't respond. He was too busy licking his plate clean, still fixated with laser focus on the meal.

Eleanor kept eating—working her way through the mashed potatoes, then on to the sliced steak. It was perfectly cooked, perfectly seasoned. The kind of dinner dreams were made of. She finished with the corn, picking up kernels one-by-one between her fingers.

When she looked up again, Charlie was done. His plate was spotless. But his eyes—hungry and pleading—were locked on her plate now.

"No, Charlie. This one's mine," she giggled, still popping corn into her mouth.

Then she paused, licking a bit of butter from her fingertip.

"You know what?" she said thoughtfully, leaning back against the pantry wall, one hand resting on her now very full stomach. "I'd really like a chocolate milkshake to wash all this down."

A sudden flash of light pulsed from the shelves, warm and quick—like a camera going off in the dark.

Eleanor flinched, shielding her eyes. Then she gasped.

Sitting neatly between her and Charlie was a tall, frosty glass, filled to the brim with a thick, creamy chocolate milkshake. A perfect swirl of whipped cream sat on top like a little cloud, and a red-and-white striped straw poked out at a cheerful tilt. Tiny beads of condensation clung to the glass, catching the soft pantry light like glitter.

Her jaw dropped, then curled into the widest grin she'd worn all day.

"Yes! Exactly what I wanted!" she squealed, grabbing the glass with both hands. She took a cautious sip, then giggled as the cold hit her tongue—rich, velvety, and just the right amount of sweet.

"Either I hit my head really hard..." she said between slurps, "or we just found what this old house was hiding all along."

She glanced down at Charlie, who was licking the last bit of mashed potatoes from his plate and looking entirely too proud of himself.

Eleanor raised her glass in a mock toast. "Charlie, I think this pantry is magic."

Charlie gave a happy ruff in agreement.

Still sipping, she turned and walked slowly out of the pantry, the milkshake leaving a sweet trail of whipped cream on her upper lip. Just before she stepped out, she looked back once more—half expecting the shelves to shimmer again.

But the pantry was still. Waiting.

Eleanor closed the door softly behind her, the click echoing like the start of a new adventure.

Chapter 5

A Town in Turmoil

Milkshake in hand, Eleanor stepped carefully over the rolled-up rug in the dining room and made her way around the corner toward the stairs. Charlie followed close behind, his paws landing in perfect sync with her footsteps.

Once inside her room, she shut the door, set her drink on the desk, and plopped into her chair. With a few quick keystrokes, she opened her laptop and launched her browser.

"The Giving Basket, Point Rock," she said aloud, typing the words into the search bar and hitting enter with an enthusiastic jab.

Tab after tab popped open—news articles, old blog posts, and dusty-looking social media pages. Eleanor devoured them one by one, scanning each for clues, links, names, dates—anything useful.

Before long, she had transformed her desk into a makeshift detective's office. A corkboard leaned against the wall, covered in post-it notes and index cards. She'd drawn timelines, scribbled arrows, circled names, and added question marks like puzzle pieces looking for their place.

"Hmm... this is interesting," she murmured, eyes darting from one thread to another. "Not one mention of the pantry. Nothing. Why?"

She paused, thinking. Then she changed tactics—adjusting her search terms and digging deeper into obscure local history, personal blogs, and myth discussion forums.

That's when she started finding stories.

Legends. Whispered memories. Bits and pieces of oral tradition. Especially those tied to the Native American tribes Mrs. Newman had mentioned in class.

The pantry wasn't anywhere online. Of course it wasn't. Something this strange, this magical, wouldn't be found in headlines or official archives.

No—this kind of truth lived between the lines. In stories passed down, reshaped, and hidden in plain sight.

The Giving Basket—that legend fit. A sacred place. Food as offering. Rituals. Rules.

Maybe it had nothing to do with her pantry.

Or maybe... it had everything to do with it.

"Aha! I think this may be it!" Eleanor shouted, springing to her feet in triumph. "This house is the Giving Basket!"

She stood there, heart pounding, a wide grin stretched across her face.

Her research had taken a turn—connecting the legend of the Giving Basket not just to the town, but to the land itself.

She scrolled through a historical article about early settlement patterns and the brutal transition that occurred as colonists moved further inland nearly four centuries ago. Language shifted. Cultures collided. Indigenous people were wiped out by disease or massacred. And with them, countless stories—entire belief systems—were lost.

But not all of them.

Some myths and traditions clung to the land, passed down through whispered stories and quiet rituals. In this part of the country, Eleanor had read, settlers often absorbed or reshaped Native beliefs into their own practices—especially through the community-centered life of the early churches.

"Hmm..." she murmured, eyes scanning another paragraph. "This article says the old church was the first building constructed in town."

She leaned back in her chair.

"Could they have built it there because of the magic?" she wondered aloud. "Did they know what this land was?"

Her mind raced.

"Could this all be real?"

She stared across the room, eyes unfocused.

"Am I going crazy?"

Eleanor continued adding notes to her research board, each new thread connecting a little more of the mystery. One discovery in particular caught her attention.

The last Native American tribe to inhabit the area had remained here into the late 1800s, long after many other tribes had been forced from surrounding lands. At the time, Point Rock was still a scattering of family farms and dirt roads. The community hadn't even been officially incorporated as a town yet.

It wasn't until after the 1940s—nearly a century later—that Point Rock began to truly grow. Subdivisions were developed, paved roads appeared, and small businesses sprang up. But one business rose above the rest.

The Henry Brothers Grocery Store.

Eleanor's parents worked there now. It was the largest business in town. And strangely, it seemed to be everywhere in her search.

Story after story mentioned it—sometimes directly, sometimes just on the edges.

There were glowing articles about how the Henry Brothers became the largest grocery chain in the region. Reports of family farms going under, unable to compete. And dozens of puff pieces about their charity work—donating food, sponsoring events, building schools and community centers. Even funding the construction of the new church, decades ago.

"It's like the town is built around this grocery store," Eleanor muttered, eyes scanning across her corkboard of index cards and threads. "Even the new church..."

She paused.

"That church was built after the old pastor was murdered," she whispered, her voice suddenly more serious. "Could there be a connection?"

She stood, pacing slightly.

"Was it really just a tragedy... or did someone know about the pantry? Did someone want to control it? Hide it? Take it?"

Her mind spun with possibilities. The original church, the murder, the Henry Brothers, the Giving Basket, the tribal traditions—they were all tangled together somehow.

And if the pantry was tied to the land, as the stories suggested, then it wasn't just a pantry.

It was a legacy.

"Eleanor, please come down for dinner!" her mother's voice called up the stairs, shattering her concentration like a thrown rock through a window.

Eleanor blinked, the spell broken.

"Whoa," she muttered. "I've been in my own world for a while."

She looked around the room. Her milkshake glass sat empty. Her laptop glowed softly in the dark. Outside the window, night had fallen.

"When did my parents even get home?" she asked, rubbing her forehead.

She shook her head and pushed back from the desk.

"Coming right down, Mom!" she called, already gathering her thoughts for what she'd do next.

Eleanor closed her laptop, slid the corkboard behind her headboard to keep it hidden from prying eyes, and headed downstairs.

She wasn't hungry—not after the steak dinner and decadent milkshake from the pantry—but she still wanted to see her parents. She had so much to tell them about the town... and about the house.

When she stepped into the dining room, she paused. The space looked different—clean. The once cluttered room now had its boxes pushed neatly to the corners, and the rolled-up rug was finally laid flat beneath the table. A simple dinner of pasta and meatballs sat steaming on their plates.

Her parents were already seated, mid-conversation, forks poking halfheartedly at their food.

"Well," her father said, "if that's what we can get from the offer, I think we should take it. Why sit in a construction zone for months? We could get another house with this money."

Eleanor's ears perked up.

"Who made an offer—and for what?" she asked, stepping fully into the room.

Her mother looked up. "One of the board members at the grocery store sent a formal request to come by and look at the house. Along with that, he made a very generous offer."

Her father nodded. "It came from Mr. Henry himself."

"Wait—Mr. Henry? As in the Mr. Henry? The owner of the grocery store?" Eleanor asked, wide-eyed.

"That's right, honey," her mother said, smiling. "Apparently he used to attend the church when he was younger. Once he found out we moved into the old rectory, he sent a letter. Said he loved the building and wanted to buy it from us."

"Yeah," her father added, "and honestly, the offer's too good to pass up."

"No. No, you can't sell the house. Not to him. Not to anyone!" Eleanor shouted, her voice sharp and urgent.

Her mother froze, fork halfway to her mouth. "Um—wha—?"

"It's a great opportunity for us to get out of this dump," her father said, clearly surprised by her outburst.

"You don't understand," Eleanor said, gripping the back of a chair. "Mr. Henry doesn't want the house because of nostalgia."

Her father leaned back, raising an eyebrow. "Oh yeah? Then what does he want it for?"

Eleanor stood, her face flushed red. "The house is magical!" she blurted.

Her parents just stared at her in complete silence.

Filling the awkward pause, Eleanor pushed forward. "Something is weird about this house. I—I don't know exactly how it works, but it's magic!"

Her mother burst into laughter. "Well, I guess the old charm of the house has gotten to our daughter," she said, turning to Eleanor's father with a smirk.

"The house is charming, sure," her mother added, "but it's also falling apart. Repairs, upgrades—it'll cost a fortune. Mr. Henry's offer is more than generous. It could set us up for the future."

"No!" Eleanor interrupted, stepping closer to the table. "You don't understand."

She looked from one parent to the other, her voice trembling with urgency. "The pantry is magic."

They blinked.

"We learned about the Giving Basket legend in school," she continued, speaking faster now. "The story says a sacred stone gave the native people the ability to summon food through prayer. What if—what if this house is connected to that? What if it's built on that same land? What if this is the Giving Basket?"

She paused, breathless. "This is why we can't sell the house!"

Her parents stared at her like she'd grown a second head.

Her dad chuckled. "Your imagination is... admirable."

"I'm not joking!" Eleanor snapped. "The pantry is magic. You can imagine a food and—poof!—it appears!"

"Charlie and I saw it happen. It happened today!"

Her father raised an eyebrow. "Eleanor..."

Her mother offered a soft, sympathetic smile. "Sweetheart, your creativity is amazing. But this opportunity—it's a once-in-a-lifetime chance. Things haven't exactly been easy for us lately. Financially... this offer changes everything."

Eleanor dropped into her chair, arms folded, mouth tight.

They didn't believe her.

Not even a little.

They were laughing.

She stared at them both, then narrowed her eyes. "I can prove it."

That got their attention.

Both parents stopped smiling.

"Okay, let's see it!" Eleanor's mother replied, her voice full of enthusiastic encouragement—with just the slightest hint of sarcasm.

Eleanor stood from her chair and took her mother's hand, practically buzzing with anticipation. She led her into the kitchen, stopping in front of the pantry door.

"Pick any food," she said. "Anything you want!"

Her mother raised an eyebrow. "Hmm... what should I wish for?" She smiled playfully. "How about dessert? Maybe something like... tiramisu?"

"That sounds perfect!"

"And while you're at it, could you conjure up an espresso too?" Eleanor's father called from the dining room, chuckling as he cleared the dishes. "I could use one right about now!"

Eleanor turned back to her mother. "Okay—just step inside, close the door, and think of the tiramisu. That's it. Just think about it."

Her mother nodded with a smirk and stepped into the pantry. The small space was lined with pantry shelves on either side and a rack of coats hanging across the back. She gave Eleanor one last amused look before shutting the door behind her.

From inside, a muffled voice could be heard. "Tiramisu. Tiramisu," she said, repeating the word like a chant. "Tira-misu... Tira-I-miss-you... Tiara-su..."

The pantry door creaked open. Eleanor's mother stepped out, still smiling—but her hands were empty.

Eleanor's heart sank.

"Sorry, honey," her mother said gently, holding up her hands. "Didn't work."

She stepped forward, brushing a stray curl from Eleanor's forehead and placing a soft hand on her shoulder. "I know this move has been a lot. And being cooped up in the house all day doesn't help. Maybe it's time to get out a bit. Try to meet some new friends, yeah?"

Eleanor stood frozen.

No dessert. No magic. No proof.

Just... disappointment.

She blinked, trying to hold it together. The corners of her mouth twitched, her fists clenched at her sides. A tight knot formed in her chest—the kind that came when you felt something important slip through your fingers and couldn't explain why no one else noticed.

But it had been real. The steak. The potatoes. The corn. The milkshake. She hadn't imagined it.

So why hadn't it worked? Did the pantry choose who it listened to? Did it... not want to be shown?

Her mother was already turning away, heading back toward the living room with a gentle sigh, as if this had all been a game Eleanor made up to pass the time.

Eleanor stared at the pantry door, still ajar, its hinges creaking slightly as it settled back into place. The shelves inside looked perfectly ordinary again—just dry goods, old coats, and shadows.

She swallowed hard.

No one believed her.

And now... she wasn't so sure she believed herself.

Just... disappointment. Cold and quiet and heavy.

A flicker of doubt crawled in at the edge of her mind, whispering the worst thought of all; Maybe it really was just my imagination.

Tears welled up in her eyes, and before she could stop them, they spilled over. "I knew it was real," she whispered. But her voice was lost under the weight of their doubt—and her own.

Overcome with frustration and heartbreak, Eleanor turned and ran—past the kitchen, past her startled father, up the groaning stairs, and into her bedroom. She slammed the door shut behind her, the echo thudding through the house like the final beat of a failed performance.

She crashed onto her bed, face buried in the pillow.

Memories of her old life—her old home, old friends—blurred together with everything that had gone wrong today. The taste of the steak still lingered in her mouth. The chill of the milkshake. It had been real. Hadn't it?

Why didn't the pantry work for her mom?

What if she was just making it up?

She thought of all the things she hadn't told her parents. How lonely the first day of school had been. How no one had saved her a seat at lunch. How she'd hadn't eaten her sandwich just so she wouldn't have to sit there longer than necessary. And now this—the one thing that felt like it belonged to her, slipping through her fingers like everything else.

Her pillow grew damp beneath her cheek. She rolled over onto her back, staring at the ceiling, eyes glassy and unfocused. In the quiet hum of the house, every creak sounded like judgment.

What if she'd broken it? What if the magic was already gone? She closed her eyes, fists curled in the blanket. I didn't mean to ruin it.

A soft wind rattled the windowpane. The shadows on the wall shifted, slow and stretching. The thoughts swirled in her mind—tangled, knotted, twisting around each other until they lost shape. Doubt. Regret. A flicker of hope. All blending together like ink dropped into water.

Then... from the depths of her drifting thoughts, a strange image began to rise. A door creaking open on its own. Shelves that reassembled themselves. Whispers behind the walls. A pantry... with no floor beneath it.

Eleanor's breathing slowed.

And just like that...

...the dream began.

Chapter 6

Tiramisu for Two

The nagging buzz of the alarm pierced through the room, landing squarely in Eleanor's ear.

She shot upright in bed like she'd been launched, hair tangled, eyes half-shut. Her heart was still pounding from a dream—one already beginning to slip away.

Something... or someone had visited her.

She couldn't remember what they looked like. There wasn't a face. No body. Not even a voice. Just a feeling—like the room had been full of someone. Like an invisible presence was standing right next to her bed, watching her. Not in a creepy way... more like waiting.

There had been warmth. A hum. A whisper, maybe—not in words, but in meaning. Like the way wind carries a thought. A message she couldn't quite grasp.

Then—gone. Wiped clean by the screech of her alarm.

Eleanor groaned, dragging herself to her feet. She rifled through her closet, tossing aside a shirt, then a sweater, then socks that didn't match. As she yanked on her clothes and wrestled her hair into something presentable, the memories of the night before hit her all over again.

The failure. The laughter. Her mom's empty hands.

Eleanor winced. The embarrassment stung worse in the daylight. She slung her backpack over her shoulder and headed downstairs.

In the kitchen, she slowed. Her eyes locked onto the pantry door. Charlie was already there—pacing, whining softly, his paws tapping at the door. He jumped up and scratched once at the wood, then looked back at her with a tilt of his head.

Like he was asking the same question she was.

"I know, Charlie," Eleanor said, her voice low. "It's real."

She glanced toward the stairwell, then leaned in closer to the pantry.

"We just need to figure out why it didn't work."

She wasn't whispering for her parents' sake—they were already gone. A paper bag sat on the counter with a note tucked under the fold. The handwriting was quick and familiar; *Not much, but something. Love, Mom.*

Eleanor stared at it for a moment, then folded the bag and tucked it into her backpack.

The pantry still hadn't moved.

But something had visited her in the night.

She could feel it.

Grabbing the brown paper bag from the counter, Eleanor listened to the familiar crinkle as she stuffed it into her backpack. She slipped on her shoes, stepped outside, and plopped down on the front step to wait for the bus.

The morning air was cool, the sky still smudged with sleepy clouds. Dew clung to the grass, and the porch wood creaked beneath her shifting weight.

Her mind wouldn't stop spinning.

Why didn't it work?

She replayed the moment again and again—her mother's playful voice inside the pantry, the careful instructions, the quiet that followed. No flash. No dessert. Just... nothing.

Charlie believed. She believed. The pantry had answered her perfectly—twice.

So what went wrong?

Was it a one-time thing? Did she imagine it after all? Or... was it something else?

She hugged her knees, brow furrowed. Maybe the pantry didn't just make food. Maybe it wasn't about wanting something. Maybe it was about needing it.

A memory flickered—how empty she'd felt after the move, how desperately she'd wanted comfort, connection, something familiar.

And then... the steak. The milkshake. Exactly what her heart had asked for.

The rumble of the bus engine rolled around the corner, pulling her out of her thoughts.

Eleanor stood slowly and boarded without a word, slipping into her usual seat in the middle. The vinyl was cold against her back, but she barely noticed. Her gaze drifted to the window as the town passed by in a blur.

Something about that pantry was alive.

And if it had rules... she was going to figure them out.

Even if it meant asking for dessert a hundred more times.

* * *

The school day passed like a blur.

Eleanor's eyes stayed fixed on her notebook, open on her desk, pages filled with scribbles and arrows and crossed-out guesses. Her teacher's voice floated in through one ear and right out the other. She barely noticed the other students, didn't raise her hand, didn't look up. Even as the first bell rang for lunch, she hardly blinked.

When the hallways emptied toward the cafeteria, Eleanor turned toward the library instead.

She carried her paper bag lunch in one hand, chewing mindlessly as she walked, determined not to waste a second. Inside the library, she found an empty table tucked away in the far corner, and sat down.

Finishing the last bite, she crumpled the bag, shoved it back into her backpack, and pulled out a folder stuffed with notes. Post-its, index cards, hand-sketched diagrams—some with stars, others with Xs, and plenty of enthusiastic doodles in the margins.

One page stood out.

A single word circled three times in the center; Tiramisu ???

"Tiramisu," she muttered to herself. "Sounds funny. But it's not... a native dish, is it?"

Her brow furrowed.

"I think it's Italian..."

She paused, remembering the restaurant they'd gone to for her parents' anniversary—the little place in the city with the checkered tablecloths and the candle in the wine bottle.

The dessert they ordered that night?

Tiramisu.

Eleanor scanned through books on Italian history, culture, and customs—but nothing mentioned the dessert.

She shifted focus, moving to the cookbook section. Her eyes caught a familiar pattern on a spine—green, white, and red stripes like the Italian flag.

Italian Desserts and Antipasto.

Eleanor's face lit up. She pulled the book from the shelf and admired the olive-green cover. An illustration of a woman rolling dough adorned the front, her sleeves dusted in flour. The book looked several decades old, like most things in the library. Its pages stuck together as if bound by time itself—gritty and stiff, like it hadn't been opened in years.

She flipped to the index, sliding her finger down the T section.

"Aha! Page 78," she whispered, a smile creeping across her face.

Turning to the page, she found the entry:

Tiramisu is a coffee-flavoured Italian dessert first introduced in America in the 1960s. Made of small layer cakes dipped in coffee, layered with a whipped mixture of eggs, sugar, and mascarpone cheese, flavoured with cocoa. The recipe has been adapted into many varieties of cakes and other desserts. Its origins are often disputed among Italian regions Veneto and Friuli Venezia Giulia.

She jotted the idea down, underlining the word twice. But the logic wobbled. "Then how did the milkshake work?" she asked aloud, brows furrowing. "That definitely wasn't some ancient recipe."

Before she could chase the thought further, a shadow stretched across the notebook.

She looked up.

"Excuse me," came a soft, polite voice just behind her.

Eleanor turned slightly, caught off guard.

"I couldn't help but notice..." the voice continued, now a little louder and unmistakably enthusiastic, "you've got books on Native American culture and Italian desserts. I don't know much about desserts—other than eating them," he added with a grin, "but I am an expert in Native American history!"

Eleanor blinked.

Standing beside her, wearing a school lanyard and clutching a clipboard like it was part of his identity, was the boy from earlier. Oliver.

"Oliver's the name," he said, straightening up, "and history is my game!"

"Shhhhh!" Eleanor hissed, holding a finger to her lips while waving her hands downward. "Why so loud? This is a library."

"Sorry!" Oliver whispered, clearly trying to tamp down his excitement. "Sometimes I get carried away when I see someone actually interested in history."

He peered at her notebook. "What are you studying? I could help you find what you're looking for—if you want."

Eleanor closed the notebook gently and looked up at him.

"Thanks," she said, polite but distant. "It's nice to see you again."

Oliver stood there waiting, hopeful.

Eleanor sighed softly and gave a small smirk. "Actually, there is something you could help me with."

"Absolutely!" Oliver beamed. "What is it?"

She slid the Italian cookbook and the folklore binder across the table.

"Put these away." She commanded in jest.

With that, she tossed her backpack over one shoulder and started walking toward the exit.

"Oh. Uh... sure," Oliver said, blinking in surprise but already gathering the books. "I'm always here—if you want to learn more. About, you know... history."

The library door closed softly behind Eleanor. Just as the end of lunch bell rang.

* * *

The final bell couldn't come fast enough.

Eleanor practically launched from her seat the moment it rang, her backpack slung over one shoulder before the sound had even finished echoing down the hallway. Her mind was already far away—back home, back in the pantry—racing through the possibilities.

Tiramisu, she thought with a thrill. What if I was right? What if it really didn't work before because the pantry didn't know it? She had memorized every detail in the library—its Italian roots, the ingredients, the era. She had even written down how to pronounce it correctly, just in case.

The walk to the bus felt like a mile. The ride itself? Pure torture. The engine droned on as they stopped at every corner, every crosswalk, every mailbox that might be mistaken for a stop. Eleanor sat motionless in her usual seat, but her thoughts buzzed like a swarm of bees. She gripped the edge of her backpack so tightly her knuckles went white.

Charlie would be waiting. The pantry would be waiting. All she had to do was get there.

Outside the bus window, Point Rock drifted by—trees, houses, signs—all brown, all dead—all a blur she didn't care to see. Her reflection in the glass looked calmer than she felt, but inside, her heart was pounding like a drum.

Just a few more blocks...And finally—finally—the bus hissed to a stop. Eleanor was up before the brakes finished squealing, half-running down the aisle and leaping down the steps, the sun warm on her face and adrenaline in her legs.

Freedom. At last.

Eleanor burst through the front door, the hinges groaning as it slammed shut behind her. She dropped her bag with a heavy thud, kicked off one shoe mid-run, and dashed straight into the kitchen. Charlie was right on her heels, skidding across the linoleum with a bark of excitement.

She didn't hesitate. She threw open the pantry door and stepped inside, the familiar creak of the hinges sending a thrill through her chest. The air inside was cool and still—almost humming with anticipation.

Charlie settled beside her, tail wagging in sweeping arcs across the floor, his nose already twitching with curiosity. Eleanor closed the door gently behind them and pressed her back against it. The shelves stood quiet and expectant, their dusty jars and stacked cans watching like silent witnesses.

"Okay," she whispered, her voice barely louder than a breath. "Let's test this theory."

She shut her eyes.

Not just any food. Not something random or modern. Something simple. Something native.

She imagined corn—not the kind from the grocery store freezer section, but real corn. Sweet summer corn, pulled fresh from a stalk still warm from the sun. She pictured the silk peeling away, the golden kernels glistening, plump and perfect. Butter melting down the sides. A touch of salt. Steam rising in lazy curls.

The air shifted.

And then—pop!

A soft, almost musical sound, like something landing gently on a plate.

Eleanor opened her eyes.

There it was.

A single, perfect ear of corn resting atop a plain ceramic dish. Still hot. Still steaming. She picked it up with both hands, breath caught in her throat, and took a bite.

The snap! echoed through the little room.

Her eyes widened. A shiver raced down her spine. It was everything she'd imagined and more—sweet, rich, earthy, buttery. She slid down to the floor in disbelief, knees pulling to her chest, as she chewed slowly, reverently. Charlie gave an approving snort and settled beside her, his chin resting on her knee.

Eleanor let the moment wash over her. This wasn't a coincidence. This wasn't imagination.

The magic was real and this house—was special.

Charlie looked at her, eyes wide in wonder. Then he slowly closed his eyes, tilted his head down, and imagined something of his own.

Moments later, a steak dinner appeared—identical to the one from the day before. Same white plate. Same layout. Perfectly replicated.

Eleanor laughed. "Go ahead—you earned it."

Charlie dug in with enthusiasm, tail wagging like crazy.

Eleanor licked the last few kernels from the cob, then leaned back, thinking. Her mind drifted to the milkshake, then to the tiramisu.

"Maybe... if I imagine the flavors instead of just the name...", she muttered.

She closed her eyes again. This time, she focused on texture. Layers. The creaminess of mascarpone. The bold taste of espresso. The faint bitterness of cocoa dusted on top. She imagined the way it would melt on her tongue; creamy, cool, with just a hint of bitterness beneath the sweetness. A dessert with elegance. Confidence. An edge.

Then—there it was. A shift in the air. A hum. A scent.

The sharp, sweet perfume of cocoa and coffee filled the pantry, rising slowly like a whisper. Eleanor's eyes snapped open.

She gasped. "What?!"

There, sitting gracefully on a porcelain dish as if served by an invisible waiter, was the tiramisu. Real. Cold. Perfect. Its layers stood tall and clean, the cocoa dusting still settling as a wisp of steam curled upward and vanished.

"Charlie—look!" she cried, voice breaking into laughter. "Tiramisu!"

She dropped to her knees in front of it, blinking fast to make sure it wasn't an illusion. Her hand hovered in the air for a beat—hesitant, reverent—then she dipped a finger into the creamy top and brought it to her lips.

One taste was all it took. She moaned. "Mmm. C'mon, have a bite!"

Charlie didn't need a second invitation. He bounded over with a happy bark, tail thumping, eyes wide with curiosity.

Eleanor grinned so wide it hurt. The rules had changed. The game was on.

Eleanor watched, still baffled, "Why didn't it work for Mom?"

She chewed her lip, thinking. Maybe... it only works for kids? But then again—Charlie had conjured food too.

Not just his own, but human food. And not from memory—but from seeing it once.

Charlie looked up from his now spotless plate, eyes gleaming with happiness.

Eleanor placed her hands on her hips, brow furrowed.

"We need answers, Charlie," she said, suddenly serious. "And I know exactly where to get them."

She paused, then sighed.

"But... we'll have to wait until tomorrow."

With a groan, she flopped backward and conjured up another chocolate milkshake—her unofficial reward for another day of magical discovery.

Chapter 7

Oliver the Know-it-all

Another unremarkable day of school was slowly dragging to its midpoint. Eleanor sat at her desk, eyes locked on the clock as the minute hand inched toward noon.

Lunch couldn't come fast enough.

She bounced her knee under the table, rehearsing lines in her head. She needed to talk to Oliver—the nerdy kid with a clipboard and too much confidence. He might be her best shot at learning more about Native American history... and the Giving Basket.

The moment the bell rang, Eleanor was already halfway out the door, backpack slung over one shoulder. She darted through the halls and slipped into the library.

It was quieter than usual. A handwritten notecard sat on the librarian's desk;

Out to Lunch — Back in 15 minutes.

No students. No noise. Just the scent of old books and waxed floors.

Eleanor moved quickly between the shelves, scanning the rows until she reached the far corner of the history section. As expected, there was Oliver—head in one hand, hunched over an open book.

"Hey," she whispered.

No response.

"Hello?" she said, slightly louder.

Still nothing.

Annoyed, Eleanor circled around the table and tapped him on the shoulder—firmly.

"Ahhh!" Oliver yelped, jolting upright so fast he nearly toppled over. "You nearly gave me a—a heart attack!" he gasped, ripping his earbuds out and tossing them onto the book in front of him.

"Oh—sorry. Didn't see the earbuds," Eleanor said, smirking. "Didn't mean to scare you. Kinda."

"You can't sneak up on people like that!" Oliver snapped, catching his breath. "I was in the middle of reading about the night raids during the fall of Constantinople and then—bam! Total panic."

"I was calling your name before I came over here," Eleanor shot back, but the edge in her voice softened.

"You… actually wanted to talk to me?" Oliver blinked. A slow smile spread across his face, replacing the scowl.

"Don't get too excited," Eleanor said, sliding into the chair across from him. "I just have a few questions. About history. Specifically the Giving Basket myth—and how it might relate to this town."

Oliver straightened instantly. "Yes! I knew you were one of us!"

Eleanor raised an eyebrow.

"Oliver's the name," he said, pointing to himself, "and history is my game."

Eleanor rolled her eyes, but the hint of a smile tugged at the corner of her mouth as she opened her notebook.

Eleanor flipped open her notebook and leaned in. "Okay, let's go over the story again," she said. "The one from class—about the Giving Basket."

Oliver nodded, eyes bright behind his glasses. "Right! It's your classic legend—mystical object, moral lesson, cultural symbolism. Nothing too specific. Most versions don't even mention a location."

Eleanor frowned, tapping her pen. "Yeah, that's what I noticed too. Do you think any of it's real? Like, do you think the Giving Basket actually existed? And if so... where do you think it would be now?"

Oliver sat up straighter, clearly energized by the question. "Well," he began, "I've got a theory."

"Of course you do," Eleanor mumbled under her breath with a half-smile.

"When settlers first arrived, the story goes that they were starving," Oliver continued. "They didn't come prepared for the winter—or maybe they underestimated how hard it would be to grow crops in the rocky soil around here. Either way, things got bad. Real bad. People were sick, frostbitten, down to boiling leather shoes just to have something to eat."

Eleanor grimaced. "Gross."

"But then," Oliver said, lowering his voice just a little, "one night, they saw fires burning beyond the tree line. The native village nearby—most likely the Wampanoag—had been watching. And according to legend, they decided to help. The chief's daughter—some stories call her Wind Song—stepped forward carrying a woven basket. She placed it at the edge of the settlement without saying a word. And when the settlers opened it... it was full of food."

Eleanor blinked. "Just like that?"

"Not just some food," Oliver said, eyes sparkling. "Enough to feed the whole colony. Bread, fruits, corn, stews—more than they could carry. Some versions say the food never ran out. Every time they reached in, there was more."

"Magical feasts on a whim," Eleanor nodded, scribbling furiously.

"But here's where it gets interesting," Oliver leaned in. "They say the basket was a gift, but with a rule; it could only be used in times of true need. Selfishness or greed would break the blessing. In one version, someone tried to take the basket for themselves—tried to hide it.

The moment they did, the food turned to ash, and the basket disappeared."

Eleanor looked up. "Disappeared?"

"Gone," Oliver confirmed. "Vanished into the earth. Some people think it was hidden. Others say it returns when the land needs it again. Like it chooses when and where to appear."

Eleanor was quiet, absorbing it all.

"So..." she said slowly, "you think the Giving Basket was real? Like, an actual object?"

Oliver shrugged, but his grin didn't fade. "Maybe not exactly how the legends say. But I think there was something. Maybe a tradition. A sacred ritual. Maybe even something... unexplainable."

"But," Oliver continued, "in my additional research, I came across something interesting. I found an old hand-drawn map of the valley—streams, rivers, trails—and overlaid it with a modern map. Guess what lines up?"

"What?"

"The rundown church."

Eleanor's eyes widened.

"From what I can tell," Oliver went on, "the native village was located exactly where that church now stands. And like with many native cultures, the tribe eventually assimilated—adopting the religion and customs of the colonists. The church may have been built directly on top of something sacred."

Eleanor scribbled quickly, her pencil nearly tearing through the page. "So... what happened to the Giving Basket?"

Oliver adjusted his glasses. "To the best of my knowledge, the Giving Basket is symbolic. A metaphor for a sacred site. Some versions of the story mention a special stone that glowed like gold and produced food through ritual."

Eleanor froze mid-word, her pencil hovering above the page. A special stone? Her mind reeled. Glowed like gold... produces food... Her thoughts raced back to the journal, to Sister Elizabeth's unfinished sentence—the one that trailed off at Sto...

She blinked. "That sounds familiar..." she murmured aloud, but her voice was distant, as if she were speaking through a tunnel. Sto... stone. It had to be. It all clicked into place like tumblers in a lock. Sister Elizabeth hadn't just been writing about food. She was writing about this. The Pantry. The Giving Basket. The Stone.

Eleanor's heart thudded. She glanced at Oliver, suddenly more certain than ever that the answers weren't just buried in folklore—they were hidden in her house. Waiting to be reawaken.

"But it could also just mean fertile land," Oliver blurted break Eleanor's deep daydream. "You know, corn is often called 'gold' in old farming records. Maybe the site just produced bumper crops year after year. That's the logical explanation, anyway."

"Huh? What do you mean by 'logical'?"

Oliver hesitated, then leaned in a little. "Well... I have some information that isn't exactly published."

Eleanor perked up.

"My great-grandfather moved here in the 1920s. I found some of his old notebooks and letters in our attic. He came to Point Rock specifically to search for the mysterious Giving Basket site."

"No way."

"Way," Oliver said proudly. "Back then, the town was tiny—basically just the church and a trading post. My great-grandfather believed the sacred site was real, and that it had something to do with that land. But... his notes suggest he never found anything."

Eleanor mulled this over. "So you think it could be real—but maybe it was just a cornfield that got paved over for the church?"

"Something like that," Oliver said, though his tone held a flicker of uncertainty.

"So... you don't believe it's real?" Eleanor asked, watching him carefully.

Oliver looked away for a second, then back at her.

"I want to," he said. "Well, the short answer is no," Oliver admitted. "But my great-grandfather claimed he saw the glowing rock with his own eyes. Then again, he was kind of an adventurer. He wrote all kinds of stories—about lost treasures and sacred sites. That's probably why I love history so much. It's like going on adventures, but through the lives of people who came before us."

Before Eleanor could respond, the piercing shrill of the bell rang through the library, cutting the conversation short.

Eleanor stood quickly and grabbed her bag. "Meet me after school at the bus line," she said. "I want to show you something that might change your mind."

Oliver blinked. "What is it?" he asked, already looking nervous.

"Come over to my house for dinner," Eleanor said as she turned to leave. "I'll show you then."

* * *

The final bell rang, signaling the end of the school day.

Students rushed out the doors like a wave breaking through the hallways. Eleanor walked steadily toward the bus line, eyes scanning the crowd—until she saw him.

Oliver.

Standing near the buses, waving his arm like he was about to fly off. His grin stretched ear to ear.

Eleanor pretended not to notice at first, but inside, she couldn't help smiling.

"Okay, okay—I see you," she said, approaching with a sigh. "You can stop waving now."

"Sorry," Oliver replied, lowering his hand. Then quickly added, "I called my house and left a message. My parents aren't home, so... they won't miss me. Maria will get the note about dinner."

"You sure?" Eleanor asked, giving him a sideways glance as she brushed past him toward the bus.

"Yup," he said, hurrying after her.

On the bus, Eleanor headed toward her usual spot in the middle. She passed a few seats, sat down, then turned back to see Oliver still standing awkwardly in the aisle.

He was frozen, overwhelmed by the sea of unfamiliar faces staring back at him.

Eleanor gave a subtle wave—then pointed to the open seat in front of her; not next to her; Bus politics.

Oliver didn't get it, but he moved forward anyway, grateful for the silent gesture.

And Eleanor? She didn't say it aloud, but she was glad he came. The bus rolled on in silence. Neither Eleanor nor Oliver spoke as they approached her stop.

Finally, Eleanor muttered, "We get off here."

She gathered her things as the bus squealed to a stop. As it pulled away, Oliver looked up at the crooked porch and peeling paint of the old house.

"This is your house?" he asked, eyebrows raised.

"Yes," Eleanor said, annoyed by his tone. "But it's not what you think. C'mon—I want to show you something amazing."

They stepped through the front door... and froze.

Eleanor hadn't expected her parents to be standing there, grinning ear to ear like they were waiting for guests at a dinner party.

"Welcome home!" her mom beamed. Then, spotting Oliver, she leaned in. "You must be Oliver. Nice to finally meet you."

Eleanor and Oliver exchanged confused glances.

Before either could speak, her mom added, "You're Mr. Henry's grandson, right? I recognize you from the pictures on his desk."

Eleanor's stomach dropped.

She turned sharply. "Wait—what's your last name again?"

Oliver blinked. "Henry. Oliver Henry."

From down the hall, her dad called out, "Oh, is Oliver staying for dinner tonight?"

"No!" Eleanor shouted, too quickly. "I—I just needed to give him something. That's all."

Her eyes were wide with panic.

Oliver looked stunned. He hadn't expected her to shut down so fast.

"I'll be right back!" Eleanor said, already turning and bolting up the stairs.

Before her parents could get a word in, she reappeared—charging back down, skipping steps as she moved. She shoved a bundle of loose notebook pages into Oliver's hands.

"Here," she said breathlessly. "Can you find more information about this?"

"Uh... sure?" Oliver replied, blinking down at the papers.

"Thanks. See you at school," Eleanor said quickly, then guided him to the door and nudged him out.

Just like that, the door closed. Oliver stood outside, baffled, staring at the wood grain in front of his nose. "...Okay?"

Inside, Eleanor's parents stared at her, speechless.

"What?" she asked, trying to sound casual—failing completely.

Her mother crossed her arms. "He could have stayed for dinner. You didn't have to be rude. You two seemed like you were getting along."

"You need friends, Eleanor," her father added. "It's nice to have someone."

Eleanor stood still, breathing heavily. Too much had hit her at once.

She looked at her mom, eyes sharp with urgency. "I need to show you something."

Chapter 8

Chef Eleanor at your Service

With her back pressed against the door, Eleanor listened to the sound of Oliver's footsteps fading down the walkway—his confused muttering trailing off like an echo.

Her heart pounded. Her thoughts raced. Everything had changed in an instant.

Oliver. Herny. Oliver Henry.

The one person she thought might understand her—the one ally she trusted—might actually be the biggest threat of all.

"I need to act fast." Eleanor thought

A plan formed almost immediately. Not a grand plan. A clever one. A dramatic one.

"I'm making dinner tonight!" Eleanor called out, spinning on her heel with sudden determination.

Her parents, still standing in the hallway, looked at her in surprise.

"This is going to be one of the finest meals you've had in a long time," she added, flashing a smile. "It's going to be... magical."

"Sure!" her mom replied with a curious grin. "What are you planning to make?"

"It's a surprise," Eleanor said, already heading toward the kitchen. "Something very special. But you'll have to wait and see."

"Sounds good to me," her father chimed in. "Should I call the burger joint in the next town over for backup?"

Eleanor's Mother paused, turned, and gave him a slow, silent nod. Just serious enough to make him laugh. "When will it be ready?" her mom asked, arching an eyebrow.

"Perfect! Just a few minutes," Eleanor said, her voice bright and rehearsed. "Head to the living room. No peeking—I mean it!"

Her parents exchanged amused glances, the kind grown-ups share when humoring a child's scheme, and ambled off toward the couch. Her dad stretched as he walked, letting out a small yawn, while her mom scooped up a throw pillow and plopped down with a content sigh. A moment later, the TV flicked on with a low hum, the evening news filling the room with soft chatter and weather maps.

Eleanor waited until they were fully settled—no sudden footsteps, no glances over the shoulder—then turned on her heel and stepped into the kitchen with purpose. It was go time!

First—pots. Then pans. Then a handful of mismatched utensils. She created a clattering symphony; bangs, clangs, clinks, and clacks. She banged the cabinet doors a little too hard. She let a spoon fall dramatically to the floor. She stirred... nothing.

All part of the act.

After a few minutes, satisfied with the performance, Eleanor took a deep breath, turned to the pantry—and stepped inside, closing the door firmly behind her.

It was time to prove it.

For real, this time.

Eleanor stood in the center of the pantry, eyes squeezed shut, heart pounding like a drum in her chest.

One shot, she told herself. Make it count.

The shelves around her stood still and silent, as if waiting.

She took a slow breath, then focused on what she knew worked—the dinner from before. The steak. The mashed potatoes. The corn. She summoned the image in her mind, sharpening it like a photograph; the golden sear of the ribeye, glistening with juices; the pillowy pile of buttery mashed potatoes with gravy pooling like satin; the sweet corn, bright and golden, still steaming, still popping gently from the heat.

She could almost taste it. Could almost feel the warmth of the plate in her hands.

Then—it happened.

A low hum rose through the floorboards beneath her feet. The air shifted, warm and rich, wrapping around her like a hug. And then came the smell—slow and savory and unmistakable.

Eleanor's eyes flew open.

There it was.

A full dinner plate floated just inches above the pantry floor, then lowered itself gently onto a folded linen napkin as if placed by invisible hands. Steam curled upward in elegant ribbons. The steak gleamed under the soft pantry light. The potatoes shimmered with melted butter. The corn glowed like treasure.

She let out a breath she hadn't realized she was holding.

It worked.

It really worked. Again.

And this time—it wasn't for her. It was for them.

"Eureka!" Eleanor shouted, then laughed to herself. "I've always wanted to say that."

A scratching sound at the door made her jump.

She paused, listening—then smiled. She knew that sound.

"Come on, Charlie," she said, opening the pantry door. "But this plate's not for you."

Charlie barreled in anyway and curled into his usual spot in the back corner. Within seconds, he closed his eyes, lowered his head—and like magic, a full bowl of dog food appeared in front of him.

Eleanor shook her head. "Show-off."

She turned back to the pantry shelves and focused again.

Another plate appeared. Identical to the first—even the grill marks on the steak were the same. The scent alone could win an award.

With a plate in each hand, Eleanor marched out of the pantry.

She set the dishes carefully on the dining room table, then poked her head into the living room.

"Dinner's ready!"

Her parents looked at each other, puzzled.

"That was... fast?" her mother said, following Eleanor to the table. But the moment she saw the food, her breath caught. "Oh my..."

"Alright, let's get this over wi—whoa!" her father said from behind. "Eleanor, this looks amazing! Where did you get this?!" His voice jumped half an octave.

"I made it," Eleanor said proudly.

They stared at her.

Then at the food.

Then back at her.

Her mother slowly took her seat, eyes wide. Her father remained standing, still blinking at the feast before him.

They picked up their utensils like they were handling fine china.

Eleanor stood nearby, watching closely, fingers twitching with nervous energy.

Her father looked at her one more time, then shrugged.

He scooped a forkful of mashed potatoes, examined the fluffy mound, and took a bite.

Like a switch being flipped, Eleanor's father froze mid-chew. His eyes went wide as he turned to stare at her.

With a mouthful of mashed potatoes, he mumbled, "Thish ish tha besh mash botadosh!"

Eleanor blinked.

He swallowed hard, set down his fork, and stared at his plate. "Wow," he said simply—then immediately shoveled another bite into his mouth.

Eleanor's mother furrowed her brow. "Did Oliver get this for you?"

"Absolutely not," Eleanor replied, her voice firm.

"Remember what I told you the other day—about this house being magical? Well..." She spread her arms. "You're tasting the magic!"

Her dad was already halfway through his meal. He dropped his fork dramatically.

"Did you put a spell on me?"

"Yes," Eleanor grinned. "You are now under my control."

Her father's eyes widened in mock terror, and Eleanor burst out laughing.

"No, the food's fine. Charlie and I already had a few plates," she said, breaking the spell of the joke.

Her mother wasn't laughing yet. "Are you sure Oliver isn't hiding in the kitchen?" she asked, eyeing the doorway. "I heard you banging pots and pans. And since when do you know how to grill a steak and make mashed potatoes from scratch?"

Eleanor's smile faded slightly. "Mom, please. Listen to me."

She looked between both of her parents.

"This house... it's actually magic. The food you're eating came from the pantry. Our pantry. I think it might be the Giving Basket from the legends we've been researching."

Her parents exchanged a look.

"Uh-huh. Is that right?" her mom said, clearly not convinced.

"Yes!" Eleanor said, more urgently now. "You have to believe me. And I can prove it."

She leaned forward. "Do you still want that tiramisu?"

Her mother chuckled, amused. "Sure. I'd love a tiramisu."

Remembering the flavor from the tiramisu she'd conjured before, Eleanor moved toward the pantry in a near trance. Her thoughts narrowed to a single point of concentration; the soft, velvety texture... the sweet, slightly bitter kick of espresso... the rich layers soaked in flavor.

She pictured the dessert from the Italian cookbook—the elegant slice, the perfect cream, the gentle dusting of spice.

That's the one, she told herself. Picture it. Taste it. Believe it.

She opened the pantry door.

There, on the shelf, sat a plain white plate—six inches wide—with a moist, perfectly cubed tiramisu resting gently at the center. A soft pyramid of whipped cream perched on top, lightly dusted with nutmeg and cinnamon.

It was flawless.

Eleanor blinked—not in disbelief that the pantry had worked, but in awe that it had recreated the exact image from her mind. Not just a dessert—the dessert.

She carefully carried the plate to the dining room.

"Here you go," she said lightly, placing it in front of her mother. "One tiramisu—just for you."

Without hesitation, her mother sliced through the layers with her fork, lifting each stratum of cake and cream like she was turning the page of a secret recipe.

She took a bite—and melted.

Her eyes closed. She leaned back in her seat and let out a soft, blissful "mmm."

"Do you like it?" Eleanor asked.

"Mmm-hmm," her mother replied through a mouthful of decadence. "This is the best tiramisu I've ever had."

Eleanor beamed.

Then—

"Wait a minute," her father said, setting his fork down and narrowing his eyes. "I see what's happening here."

Eleanor turned.

"You had your mom wish for tiramisu the other night," he continued. "This was a setup. You already had this planned. We walked right into your trap."

He crossed his arms, raising a skeptical brow.

"No, I promise!" Eleanor snapped, stepping forward with conviction. "How about you think of something—and I'll get it for you!"

Her father raised an eyebrow. "Alright, hmm..."

He rubbed his chin, clearly searching for something out there.

"Do you remember those lobster rolls we had in Maine? At the harbor place with the picnic tables? I've been dreaming about them all summer. I'd love to have one of those again."

He chuckled, then sighed. "So go on, magic house—do your thing and bring me back that roll."

Eleanor grinned.

She remembered it perfectly. The soft, toasted bun. The warm lobster drenched in lemon butter. Even she had loved it—and she didn't even like seafood.

She closed her eyes.

She pictured the beach, the paper tray, the cold lemonade in her hand. Her family all laughing together. She locked onto the taste, the smell, the exact feel of that perfect bite.

She opened the pantry door.

And burst out laughing.

Not only was the lobster roll sitting there—perfectly wrapped, still warm—but beside it sat a golden heap of fries and a large paper basket of clam cakes.

"How did this get here?" Eleanor whispered, eyes wide. "I must've imagined the whole meal without even meaning to!"

She carried the plate proudly back to the table, placing the lobster roll in front of her father.

"The clam cakes are on me," she added, tossing the basket into the center of the table with a grin.

Her parents stared in stunned silence.

This wasn't just a good dinner. This wasn't just a trick. They were miles from the nearest restaurant that could make anything close to this. There was no way. No shortcut. No sleight of hand. Only one explanation.

The pantry... has magical powers.

"I—I can't believe it," her father whispered. "How is this even possible?"

Eleanor smirked. "There's no way I pre-ordered this one."

She turned back toward the kitchen. "I'm getting myself a milkshake. Anyone else want one?"

Her father took one bite—and froze.

Then leaned back in his chair, eyes closed in bliss.

He chewed slowly, reverently. "This... is the most amazing thing I've ever tasted."

With his mouth still full, he added, "You have to show us how this works."

Chapter 9

An Illuminating Experience

Eleanor, brimming with confidence, raced into the kitchen and flung open the pantry door.

She reached up and pulled down an armful of coats from the overhead rack, tossing them into a heap. Then she scooped up the once-neatly arranged shoes and flung them into a disorganized pile in the middle of the kitchen. Finally, she grabbed the mop and broom from the far corner beside the shelves and leaned them near the dining room wall, out of the way.

"C'mon now!" she called out over her shoulder. "There's more room now!"

With a satisfied twirl, she slipped into the pantry.

Her parents followed—along with Charlie, whose tail wagged with excitement—until all four were shoulder to shoulder in the tight space. The pantry was now packed wall to wall with family and questions.

Eleanor crouched down beside Charlie to give her parents a little more breathing room.

"Now what?" her mother asked, clearly skeptical but curious.

"Now," Eleanor said, already settling into her practiced routine, "you imagine a food. Any food. Picture it in your mind. Really focus on it. And if you do it right—it shows up."

Her parents exchanged doubtful glances.

"I'll go first," Eleanor said confidently. "The pantry makes fantastic chocolate milkshakes."

She tucked her head between her knees, closed her eyes, and stretched one hand out into the open space. She pictured the cold glass, the rich chocolate, the swirl of whipped cream, the striped red-and-white straw.

And then—she felt it.

Her fingers curled around the cold condensation of the glass.

She opened her eyes.

Her parents stared in stunned silence.

"See?" Eleanor said, raising the milkshake like a trophy. "Told you."

She took a slow, smug sip, the straw squeaking softly.

"I—I don't believe it," her father muttered, his eyes still locked on the floating miracle in her hand.

"It's right there," her mother added, stepping back slightly. "What is this place?"

The question hung in the air, thick with wonder—and something else, the realization that everything was about to change.

"You just imagine something you want, and it appears right in front of you!" Eleanor said, grinning from ear to ear.

Her father squinted. "Does it only work on food, or... can we imagine anything?"

Eleanor shrugged. "I'm not sure. You could try something else—see what happens."

Her father accepted the challenge with a dramatic breath. "Alright, let's give this a shot."

He closed his eyes tightly, forehead scrunching in deep concentration. Holding out one hand, he focused.

"I'm thinking of something very unique... very expensive..."

Seconds passed.

Then—with a soft pop—something landed in his hand.

He opened his eyes and laughed. "Wow!"

In his palm sat a king-sized candy bar, wrapped in shiny red foil.

Eleanor peered over. "But... that's still food."

Her father unwrapped it and took a generous bite, the caramel stretching with each chew.

"Well," he said, mouth half-full, "I started with that Swiss dive watch I've been wanting for years. But when it didn't work, I figured... eh, might as well go for candy."

He licked some melted chocolate from his thumb. "This is really good, though."

"So I guess... it can only make food," Eleanor's mother said, eyes scanning the small room. "That's the rule?" She looked at Eleanor. "Is this why Mr. Henry wants the house so badly?"

Eleanor nodded slowly and shrugged. "It makes sense."

Her father chimed in again, bits of peanut still in his teeth. "Maybe he wants to sell the food at the store. Imagine what this could do for business." He swallowed the last bite with a dramatic gulp and patted his stomach. "I'd buy it."

"I agree," Eleanor's mother said, concern tightening her voice. "Maybe we should reconsider the offer—or at least extend the deadline so we have time to figure out what to do."

She looked down at her hands, then back at Eleanor. "This is... a lot of power. And with great power comes great responsibility."

Eleanor raised an eyebrow. "Isn't that Spider-Man?"

Her father grinned. "Hey, I was just thinking the same thing."

Then he sobered. "But she's right. We need to schedule a meeting with Mr. Henry. Soon. I just wish there was some kind of instruction manual or something." He brushed crumbs from his hands and let out a breath.

And then—it happened.

A sudden glow began to pulse beneath the pantry floorboards.

Golden-white light streamed through the seams in the wood, spilling into the room like dawn breaking through shutters. Dust swirled upward in tiny spirals, catching the glow and dancing like fireflies.

A soft, low hum pulsed from the floor. A rhythm.

Like a heartbeat.

"What is that?" Eleanor cried, leaping to her feet.

The light grew brighter.

"Everybody out!" her father ordered, swinging open the door.

They all scrambled back, crowding just outside the pantry.

Charlie didn't move. He stood in the center of the glow, pawing at the floor. Scratching. Digging.

With each scrape of his claws, the light pulsed—once, then twice—as if responding to him.

And then, the vibrations started.

First the floor. Then the shelves. Then their bones.

The rhythm—steady, slow, and powerful—spread through them like a drumbeat under their skin.

It wasn't frightening.

It was... calming.

A strange, almost sacred stillness settled over the family. No one spoke. They simply watched, listened, and felt.

The pantry wasn't just showing them something.

It was calling to them.

"I'll be right back," Eleanor's father said, then stepped out of the room.

A few moments later, he returned—carrying a large hammer.

He met Eleanor's eyes and said calmly, "Don't worry. The rock... it asked me to do this."

He gently moved Charlie out of the way, then knelt and traced the glowing floorboards with his fingers, as if marking the spot.

With a single, deliberate swing, he brought the hammer down.

THUD.

A splinter snapped into the air. Nails squealed as they were pried loose from the old wood. The sound of wood giving way echoed in the tight space, raw and resonant.

One by one, the nails were removed. Finally, the board came free in a single clean piece—like it had been placed there intentionally, waiting to be uncovered.

Beneath it, the glow intensified.

The family leaned in, peering into the radiant void below.

"Careful!" Eleanor's mother called, her hand instinctively reaching forward.

"There's something down there," her father murmured, eyes locked on the light. "Something... pulsing."

It was milky white—crystal-like, yet clouded. It shimmered with a liquid sheen, almost alive. Golden light pulsed from within it, not just illuminating but radiating, as if warmed from the inside by a silent fire.

Its surface shimmered in swirls that constantly changed, never the same from one moment to the next. A large stone, fixated to the bedrock under the house.

But that wasn't all.

Also pulled from the hole was a staff, roughly two feet long. Clearly made of wood, but worn smooth with age. Intricate carvings spiraled around both ends—one light, the other dark.

"Look at this," Eleanor's father breathed. "There are markings all over it."

He held it to the light, turning it carefully in his hands, watching the carved symbols shift with each rotation.

"What could it be?" Eleanor's mother asked, leaning in over his shoulder.

"Here—this one looks like the stone," he said, pointing to a symbol. "And these... look like crops. Wheat. Maybe water? This is food—life."

He rotated the staff again.

"But look at the bottom," Eleanor said, her voice suddenly quiet. "Below the zig-zag lines... that doesn't look so pleasant."

Her words hung in the air.

The staff told a story—two halves of it. One end was natural wood, carved with symbols of prosperity; full fields, clean water, fruit, and sun. A world in balance. But the other end was charred black, scorched by fire. The carvings were deeper here—etched violently. A figure loomed at the center; twisted, monstrous. A demon of sorts.

It held a sickle in one hand, flames in the other.

It destroyed the crops. Boiled the water. Burned the land.

Eleanor took a step back, uneasy.

"What... is this?" she whispered.

Her father didn't answer.

No one did.

They just stood there, the faint glow of the stone reflecting in their eyes.

"What do you think this means?" Eleanor asked, watching her parents as they studied the symbols carved into the staff—still trying to decipher its message.

Her father rotated the staff slowly in his hands. "Well, we can clearly see there's a duality here. Light wood on one end, blackened and charred on the other... Could this be a metaphor?"

He paused, thinking aloud. "I remember reading about ancient civilizations—nearly all of them structured belief systems around opposing forces."

"Opposing forces?" Eleanor repeated.

"Yeah. Light and dark. Good and evil. Heaven and hell. There's even an old saying; as above, so below." He turned the staff again, watching the carvings catch the pantry's soft light. "This staff might be a warning. An omen to anyone who finds the stone."

"So... you think this could affect the town, too?" Eleanor's mother asked, her voice quiet.

"Perhaps," he replied.

Eleanor stepped closer. "What if those deserted farms just a few miles from here—the ones with dried-up soil and dead crops—what if they're a result of the magic being misused?"

Her parents both turned to her.

"What if the bad magic... spreads?" she continued. "This could be a message not to abuse the pantry. Maybe the dark end of the staff is what happens when the balance is broken."

"Very astute, Eleanor," her mother said, clearly impressed.

"You may have a point," her father added. "But one thing's for certain—this stone, and whatever it's tied to, must be protected. No one else can know about it."

Eleanor shifted uncomfortably. "Well... I may have already spoiled that."

Her parents stiffened.

"What do you mean?" her father asked. Both parents locked eyes on her.

"You remember Oliver?" Eleanor said, glancing away. "I may have given him some notes. Stuff I found in the house. I didn't know he was related to Mr. Henry, and I definitely didn't realize how serious this all was at the time."

She walked slowly back toward the dining room.

"What kind of information?" her mother asked.

Eleanor paused, then turned.

"This may go way deeper than just a magic stone or an old pantry," she said. "The previous owner of this house—Pastor Holland—I think he was the guardian of the stone. A protector." "But... he was murdered," she added quietly. "And the land was only ever entrusted to those who served in the church."

Her father nodded solemnly. "Yes. That was your grandfather."

Eleanor looked at them both. "And now that they're gone... maybe it's us. Maybe we've been chosen to protect it next."

Her mother frowned. "But what does Oliver have to do with all this?"

"The notebook I gave him," Eleanor replied, her voice growing firmer, "was from one of the church's former members. And the biggest clues? They're in the old newspaper articles I found in the library. There's more going on than we think."

She pointed to the dining room table. "Please, sit down. I'll show you everything."

Her parents pulled out the chairs, sitting without a word.

Eleanor laid out her notes—maps, old letters, sketches, names from the journal, newspaper clippings. She explained the history of the house, the role of the pastor, the crime, and the strange trail of inheritance that led to them.

They stayed up talking for hours—piecing together a puzzle no one else even knew existed.

And sometime after midnight, with her notes spread out and her eyes barely staying open, Eleanor curled up on the couch—exhausted.

She fell asleep surrounded by questions...

...but no longer alone in trying to answer them.

Chapter 10

A Kid in Big Trouble

Eagerly waiting for the lunch bell to ring, Eleanor sat at her desk, foot tapping, fingers drumming. Her impatience was second only to her excitement. She couldn't stop thinking about the Giving Basket, the pantry, and—most of all—the strange carved staff beneath her house.

If anyone could help her decode the meaning behind the symbols she'd copied into her notebook, it was Oliver—the self-proclaimed historical expert. He might even know how it all tied into the land itself.

Maybe he's seen these symbols before.

The bell finally rang with a steady, resonant tone.

Eleanor shot from her seat before anyone else had even stood up, backpack half-zipped as she sped down the hall. She pushed through the library doors and made a beeline for the back tables.

Sure enough, there was Oliver—already deep into a book, with three more stacked beside him.

He didn't notice her at first, too engrossed in the text. It wasn't until Eleanor's shadow grew large across the open pages that he looked up.

"Eleanor!" he said, clearly surprised. "I've got some ideas for you."

He smiled as he cleared the stack of books, shifting them onto the chair beside him where his bookbag sat slumped. Then, rummaging quickly through the bag, he pulled out Eleanor's notes and laid them gently on the table between them.

"I think you're on to something," he said, tapping the papers with a satisfied nod.

The notes were scattered pages from Eleanor's notebook—copies of Sister Elizabeth's letters to the town, annotated and color-coded with sticky note tabs. Each tab was labeled with a number corresponding to Oliver's own cross-referenced notes.

"I found something that might sound outrageous," Oliver blurted, barely letting Eleanor sit down. "But I think your house might be the original location of the Giving Basket!"

Eleanor reached for the notes, but Oliver was already pulling out another document—a neatly typed and printed sheet of paper, covered in numbered footnotes, underlined references, and clean citations.

"I made notations to match your copies," he said, spreading them side by side. "You can see the links right here."

"Wait—you found all this just from my notes?" Eleanor asked, stunned.

"I stayed up all night trying to piece it together," Oliver admitted, lowering his voice. "And... I know my grandfather is trying to buy your house. I overheard some of the discussions over dinner the other night."

He paused, glancing around to make sure no one was listening. "He wants to restore the church. Renovate it—bring it back to its original form. But here's the strange part; the original agreement for the property said it could only be sold to a handful of specific parishioners."

Oliver flipped a few pages and pointed to a highlighted line. "After the pastor was murdered... something changed. A drought hit the valley. People got sick. The farms failed. Within a few months, most of the town had cleared out."

"What?" Eleanor said, her voice echoing just a bit too loud. "You mean to tell me that after the pastor died, the town started to—"

"Shhh!" Oliver hissed, glancing toward the librarian's desk. "This is still a library."

Eleanor leaned in, still wide-eyed.

"But yes," Oliver whispered. "There seems to be this... odd pattern. A coincidence, maybe. But it lines up. Pastor dies. Farms go dry. Town fades. That's probably why the house sat empty until you moved in."

Eleanor was still trying to catch up, but Oliver wasn't finished.

"The weirdest part? My family—the Henrys—were part of the church too. But they were excluded from the original agreement." He furrowed his brow. "I don't know why. And no one in my family talks about it."

"Excuse me?" came a voice from the other side of the bookshelf.

Eleanor and Oliver froze. They turned in unison, eyes locking on the narrow gaps between the books. A slow movement on the other side—shifting shadows, the creak of a sensible shoe—signaled someone approaching. Through the slivers between the shelves, a familiar, gentle face leaned into view.

It was the librarian. Of course it was the librarian.

She stepped forward slowly, a faint smile playing at her lips. "I think I can answer that question for you, dear," she said softly, her voice warm but edged with something knowing. She didn't need a library card to be everywhere at once. She was the library.

Eleanor blinked. "You were listening?"

The librarian chuckled lightly, brushing invisible dust from the front of her blouse. "Old libraries have thin walls—and old librarians have sharper ears than you think. Especially when students start poking around in town legends and family histories."

She stepped fully into view now, standing at the head of their table, hands folded neatly in front of her.

"What do you mean?" Eleanor asked, her voice more curious than alarmed.

"Well," the librarian said, lowering her voice and glancing over her shoulder, "it's a bit of a long story. And some of the details are foggy by now." Her eyes shifted to Oliver with a look that seemed to read him like a book. "But I do remember your family being removed from the church... due to an incident. It happened just before the tragic death of the pastor."

Oliver sat up straighter. "How so?"

The librarian hesitated, fingers lightly brushing the edge of the table, as if weighing the past in her hands. Then she leaned in, her voice softening to a near-whisper.

"Your great-grandfather and his brother were caught in the rectory kitchen—stealing food. And not just stealing," she added, with a knowing glance. "It was a disaster. Pots overturned, flour in the air, preserves shattered on the floor. One story claims they were trying to make a cake out of communion bread and wine. Another says they were searching for something specific—something hidden behind the walls."

Oliver's brow furrowed. "What were they looking for?"

The librarian shook her head slowly. "No one ever knew for sure. The boys didn't talk about it much. Not then, and not later in life."

She trailed off for a moment, her voice tightening.

"They say things started going wrong after that night. The church pantry was sealed up. The pastor fell ill soon after and passed away within the month. And your family—Oliver—was quietly removed from church service. No scandal. No accusations. Just... gone. Like the town agreed to forget."

Eleanor sat motionless, goosebumps rising on her arms.

The librarian's voice dropped even lower. "Some people chalked it up to superstition. Others swore the church was hiding something nefarious. But your great-grandfather... he always said the truth was somewhere in between."

She leaned back, her gaze calm but piercing. "And now here you are, asking the same questions."

"That's it?" Oliver blinked. "They were kicked out for that?"

The librarian gave a faint smile, something unreadable in her expression. "There's more to it, sweetheart," she said, eyes glinting. "There's always more."

She looked around again—more cautiously this time—then leaned closer. "I was friends with your grandfather. We were in school together. He told a few of us kids what really happened that day."

She paused, lips pressed tight.

"I don't know if I should be telling you this," she added, pulling back slightly, clearly conflicted.

"No—please," Eleanor said, sitting up straighter. "We need to know."

The librarian hesitated for another long second. Then, with a sigh, she eased into the chair beside them, folded her arms, and took a long, steady breath. She closed her eyes. Her lips moved at first with no sound—as if she were deciding how much to say, or whether to say anything at all.

Finally, her voice returned. "Alright," she said, her tone shifting. "But promise me—do not repeat this to your grandfather, Oliver. No need to dredge up ghosts that don't want waking."

Oliver nodded quickly. "We promise."

The librarian leaned in.

"After the incident in the kitchen, your grandfather started telling these wild stories. They were... fantastical. He claimed the kitchen had a never-ending supply of energy. Not electricity or tricks of the eye, but real power. The kind that comes from somewhere else. According to him, the brothers didn't stumble into the kitchen by accident—they'd overheard whispers. Grown-ups talking in hushed tones about a space that could answer hunger with a wish. A space that once fed a congregation during a harsh winter with no supplies.

She continued, "Thats what happened when his father and uncle went in that day; food just kept appearing. Meats, pies, drinks—everything. He said it filled the room to the ceiling." Her eyes twinkled. "By the time the pastor found them, the rectory was so overstuffed, food was spilling into the hallways. He said the kitchen was alive."

Oliver stared at her, mouth half open.

"That's why they were removed from the parish?" Eleanor asked.

The librarian's smile faded.

"There's a bit more to the story, my dear," she said quietly.

Her tone darkened. "The incident happened about a week before the pastor's death. And after he died, there were... mysterious circumstances involving your granduncle." She turned slightly, not looking at Oliver.

"What circumstances?" Oliver asked, his voice tinged with concern.

The librarian took a slow, deep breath, then exhaled softly. "Your grand-uncle left town just a few days after the incident," she said. "There was a lot of backlash... rumors. He was accused—unofficially—of killing the pastor."

Her eyes dimmed with the memory.

"Later, the authorities found the culprit; a drifter passing through town. I was only twelve then. I didn't fully understand what had happened. But... your grand-uncle never returned."

She looked to Oliver gently.

"I'm sure it was all a misunderstanding, sweetheart. Your family's always been good people."

She stood up slowly, brushing off her skirt.

"That's all I remember," she added. "Be careful, you two."

Without another word, she turned and walked away, leaving them alone in the stillness of the library.

Eleanor and Oliver sat frozen—each staring at the other, minds spinning.

The bell rang, signaling the end of lunch. But neither of them moved. They remained at the table, silent... locked in a gaze that held far more questions than answers.

Finally, Oliver spoke, just above a whisper. "I'm going to get answers."

Chapter 11

A Grand Old Story

Immediately after school, Eleanor and Oliver skipped the bus and decided to walk to the Henry Brothers Grocery store in search of answers.

The awkward silence from the library trailed after them like a long, dark shadow—stretching between their footsteps, weighing down the space between every word left unsaid. The sky above seemed to mimic the mood; gray, low-hanging clouds gathering like whispers of a coming storm. A quiet wind tugged at their jackets and rustled the leaves along the sidewalk, but neither of them spoke.

Oliver walked with his hands in his pockets, eyes on the ground. He didn't offer one of his usual facts or jokes, didn't even glance sideways. A storm cloud hovered over him—both literal and emotional—as if something unseen were following, clinging to his back.

Eleanor, not one to press, matched his pace, her arms crossed tightly across her chest. Her thoughts churned like water in a jar. The librarian's words had cracked something open in her; the pantry was real. The Giving Basket was real. But so were the rumors. The warnings. The possibility of something darker.

The pastor's death. The family exile. The food that turned to ash.

She had felt the magic—had tasted it. But now... it felt heavier. As if behind every wish granted, something else was watching. Waiting.

And Oliver. Sweet, clipboard-carrying Oliver. Could she still trust him? Her eyes flicked sideways, studying his hunched shoulders and the furrow in his brow. He wasn't joking now. He wasn't leading or theorizing or spinning wild ideas. He was quiet. Heavy. Guilty?

She looked away quickly, guilt of her own blooming in her chest. It wasn't fair to doubt him. He hadn't done anything wrong. But what if his family had?

Finally, Oliver broke the silence.

"Do you think any of this is true?" he asked, his voice low.

"I don't know," Eleanor answered quickly, careful not to lead him one way or the other.

"Eleanor?" he asked again, this time more quietly.

"Yes?" she said, pausing as he slowed to a stop.

He turned to her, head lowered, eyes wide behind his glasses.

"Thank you... for coming with me today," Oliver said, offering her a faint, sincere smile before continuing on.

Eleanor gave a quiet nod and fell in step beside him.

They wandered down cracked sidewalks, their footsteps out of rhythm but somehow in sync. The silence between them softened—not gone, but less jagged. They kicked at loose gravel and crumbled acorns, letting the sound fill the empty air. Bits of nature became tools for distraction. Oliver stooped to gather a handful of small, flat stones, flicking them at tree trunks with focused precision. Each thunk echoed like a tiny triumph, a way to push back the unease.

Eleanor, meanwhile, found a long, crooked branch in the grass. She twirled it once, then held it high like a wizard's staff, lifting it toward a telephone pole. "Your power is mine!" she declared, her voice theatrical. A squirrel darted by, and she pointed her staff with mock intensity. "You shall not pass!"

Oliver cracked a smile. He picked up a pinecone and lobbed it gently into a bush. "Dark forces vanquished."

Eleanor grinned, swinging her staff like a sword. They leapt over sidewalk cracks, ducked under low-hanging branches, and for a moment—just a moment—it felt like they had stepped outside of time. No mysteries. No family legacies. Just two kids chasing shadows and casting spells into the wind.

But as the red-and-white sign of the Henry Brothers Grocery store rose above the trees, its flickering light cutting through the gray sky, the weight returned—swift and sudden, like a curtain falling.

They reached the edge of the parking lot and stopped.

Eleanor looked down at the branch in her hand. The magic was gone. It was just a stick now. She dropped it into the brush.

Oliver stared ahead, then quietly let the last of his stones fall from his palm. He turned to her, his expression unreadable, and gently reached out, placing a hand on her arm.

"Hey," he said quietly. "Can we keep all this between us? I don't want to give the other kids more ammo. You're... the only one who actually talks to me."

Eleanor hesitated for a heartbeat, then nodded. "Of course."

"Thanks," Oliver said, the cheer briefly returning to his voice. Then his expression grew serious again. "To be honest, I'm kinda scared to ask my grandfather about all this. But... I have to know."

"The truth is the truth," Eleanor said, sounding almost like him now. "It doesn't change just because it's uncomfortable."

Oliver laughed once under his breath. "You're right."

They walked toward the store entrance.

"Will you be hanging around?" he asked.

"No," Eleanor said. "My parents' shift is almost over. I'll probably catch a ride with them in about an hour."

"Okay," Oliver nodded. "Today's been... heavy. I'll see you in school tomorrow. Hopefully."

He took a deep breath, squared his shoulders, and disappeared down the hallway toward the manager's office. Oliver turned back once more at the end of the hallway. He caught Eleanor's eye, gave her a nervous smile and a wave, then adjusted his glasses, parted his hair with one hand, and puffed out his chest.

He knocked three times on the office door, steady and deliberate, holding his breath as he did.

"Come in!" a deep voice called from within.

Oliver opened the door.

"Oliver! What a nice surprise," his grandfather said warmly. "Come on in, take a seat." He closed his laptop with a gentle click, giving Oliver his full attention. "To what do I owe the honor?"

"Hi, Grandpa," Oliver said, his voice small at first. "I wanted to ask you something... about when you were a kid."

His tone grew stronger with the second sentence.

His grandfather leaned back slightly. "Sure, what do you want to know?"

"Well," Oliver began, "I've been researching the history of Point Rock, and I came across a story. One that involves... our family. And the old church."

That caught his grandfather's attention. The older man stood slowly, walked around to the front of his desk, and sat on the edge—facing Oliver directly.

"I think I know where this is going," he said carefully. "Is this about our exile from the church?"

"Yes," Oliver replied. "But also... the Giving Basket."

That did it.

His grandfather's posture shifted. The casual warmth faded. He stood silently for a moment, then retreated back behind the desk and lowered himself into his chair with a slow exhale.

"Wow," he said at last. "Okay... that's a lot to unpack." He rested his hands on the desk. "Why don't you start by telling me what you already know," his grandfather said calmly, folding his hands. "And I'll fill in the rest."

So Oliver did.

He spoke slowly at first, cautiously laying out the pieces. The legend of the Giving Basket. The story of the pantry. The rumors that stretched back generations. He chose his words with care—deliberate, practiced—careful not to mention Eleanor or the librarian by name. He left out the journal. Left out the magic. But the bones of the story were there.

His grandfather didn't move. Didn't interrupt. He sat in his high-backed chair like a statue carved from memory, his face unreadable, his eyes locked on Oliver. No nods, no questions. Just listening. Letting the room fill with the weight of everything that had been unspoken for decades.

Oliver's voice faltered once—when he mentioned the kitchen incident, the rectory mess, the supposed exile—but he pressed on. When he finally reached the end, he trailed off into silence, feeling the air between them tighten like a drawn string.

He leaned forward, heart pounding. "So..." he said, barely above a whisper, "is it true?"

For a moment, his grandfather didn't answer. The clock on the wall ticked loudly. Somewhere outside, a bird called. The silence stretched just long enough to sting. Then the old man shifted in his seat, the leather creaking beneath him. He looked not at Oliver, but at the far wall—as if memory itself had returned and taken shape in the room.

"Is the Giving Basket real?" Oliver asked, eyes locked on his grandfather.

The silence in the room thickened, heavy with tension.

Then—laughter.

A booming, belly-deep laugh erupted from Oliver's grandfather as he pushed back his chair and stood up. With surprising energy, he crossed the room to a tall bookshelf and scanned the spines.

"Let's see here..." he muttered, eyes flicking across the leather-bound volumes. Then he reached up and pulled down a dark grey book, its edges lined in gold.

"Take a look at this," he said, placing the book gently in Oliver's lap. With a small bounce in his step, he returned to his desk and sat down with a look of fond memory in his eyes.

"What is this?" Oliver asked, holding the heavy ledger with care.

"I see you've been reading from my father's journals," his grandfather said. "A lot of those stories were just that—stories. But this one... this one is different."

He leaned forward.

"You see, my father and his brother weren't just troublemakers—they were treasure hunters. Amateur, of course. Inspired by the great expeditions to Africa and Asia during their youth."

He smiled, the pride in his voice unmistakable.

"They stumbled across a mention of a magical stone buried deep in the ship logs held in the Ashmolean Museum in Oxford. The stories were vague—partial translations, unclear references—but it was enough to spark a lifelong search."

Oliver's brow furrowed. "But what does that have to do with the church? With this town?"

His grandfather raised a finger, the corners of his mouth curling into a knowing smile.

"Patience, young Mr. Henry," he said, his voice low and edged with excitement. "My father later came across another ship's log—this one from a voyage to the New World in 1698. A man named Captain Verdensun."

He pushed back from the desk slightly and gestured to the large, yellowed map on the wall behind him—edges curling, pins scattered like breadcrumbs across the terrain.

"According to the log, Verdensun described a strange land hidden beyond the coast. A valley surrounded by thick woods. And within it—a stone. A radiant stone, said to be guarded by the native people. One that could produce... not gold or silver, but sustenance. Provisions. Enough to fill ships."

Oliver leaned in, eyes wide.

"But the captain died on the return voyage the following year. Fever, supposedly. The log never reached England. No official record. No royal charter. Just pages in a dusty box, half-eaten by time."

He paused, letting the weight of the silence speak for itself.

"But my father," the old man said, his voice dropping, "he believed he'd uncovered something important. Something sacred."

Oliver flipped open the gray ledger on the desk, fingers trembling slightly. His breath caught as he landed on a page deep inside—a hand-drawn sketch, faded but still striking. It showed a glowing stone, emitting curved lines of light. Two Native Americans stood beside it, offering plates of food. Beside them, a man—labeled Verdensun—overlooked a stockpile of barrels and crates being loaded onto a ship.

"You mean to tell me..." Oliver whispered, voice almost cracking, "the magical rock is the Giving Basket?"

His grandfather nodded slowly, his eyes distant.

"That's what your great-grandfather and great-uncle believed. They followed the trail—every log, every rumor. Crossed the ocean, stowaway in a cargo ship and settled here in 1937 as young boys, convinced this valley held the truth. Not just of a story—but of something real. Something buried. Something waiting."

"But did they ever find it?" Oliver asked.

"Not quite," his grandfather said, sighing deeply. "When they arrived, the stone was nowhere to be found. But over time—after years of listening to the town's stories, the myths, the rumors—they came to believe it had been hidden beneath the church. That it was built directly over it."

He pointed to the ledger still open in Oliver's lap.

"Turn to the last few pages."

"Is this a picture of your father and uncle?" Oliver asked, pointing to a faded black-and-white photo tucked into the final pages of the ledger. Two gentlemen stood proudly in front of a weathered brick building.

"Indeed, young Mr. Henry!" his grandfather said with pride. "That's them. This was taken in front of the original Henry Brothers Grocery Store. 1955 if I remember correctly."

He smiled briefly. "They created it in honor of the Giving Basket legend."

Then, his tone softened.

"But over the next twenty years or so, my father poured himself into the store. He stopped talking about the legend. Eventually, he gave up the search for the magical stone entirely."

His voice trailed off as he slumped back into his chair, the weight of memory pressing down on him.

"So... the magical stone from the ship logs," Oliver asked slowly, "is the same as the Giving Basket?"

His grandfather nodded, still looking down. "One and the same."

"For decades, its magic was hidden—buried beneath the church, preserved only in myth. But not everyone let it go."

He sat up just slightly, his voice lowering.

"My uncle was... different. He never gave up. He believed."

A beat passed. Then he added, "When I was young, I broke into the church rectory to see for myself."

Oliver's eyes widened.

"My uncle used to supply the church with food for their annual barbecue. One year, while unloading groceries into the rectory kitchen... he found something."

He looked at Oliver now, really looked at him.

"He said the pantry was built directly over the rock. He was certain. One day, while dropping off supplies, he opened one of the bags—just a regular grocery bag—and food just... kept coming out. An endless supply. Loaves of bread. Bunches of grapes. Whole hams. He said it was like the bag wasn't emptying."

He paused again, this time sitting upright with purpose.

"My uncle tried to convince my father to leverage the store—to buy the church and rectory outright. Said we could be caretakers. Guardians. But my father wouldn't hear of it."

He took a moment and shook his head.

"At the time, the church still mattered to the community and my father had lost the stomach for treasure hunting. He wanted to build something real."

He folded his hands.

"And so... the rock stayed hidden. The story faded. Until now."

Oliver sat in stunned silence, hands still clutching the ledger.

Finally, he asked the question again—softer this time.

"Is the Giving Basket... real?"

Standing up from his chair, Oliver's grandfather leaned across the desk and lowered his voice.

"Oliver, you need to keep this between us. Just us." He straightened, his voice rising with emotion. "I've seen your passion—for history, for adventure, for the truth. You've got the same fire my father and uncle once had. The same fire I had, too... once."

Oliver's brow furrowed. "What do you mean?"

His grandfather took a slow breath.

"I was around your age when I first walked past the church and rectory. I noticed the rectory door was open. I went in, looking for the pastor, but he wasn't there. So I... wandered."

He looked down, ashamed.

"I snuck into the kitchen," his grandfather said quietly, the words curling like smoke in the stillness of the room. "And then into the pantry. I wanted to see if my uncle's stories were true—about the stone, the Giving Basket, the journals, the ship logs. My father wanted nothing to do with it. Said it was superstition. Said it brought nothing but trouble."

He paused, his eyes losing focus—gazing not at Oliver, but at something distant, something remembered.

"But I had to know."

For a moment, he smiled—faint, almost boyish.

"I was skeptical, of course. I figured, if there was anything to it, it would take more than belief. I poked around. Ran my fingers along the shelves. Nothing unusual. Just canned beans and dusty tins. But then... I got hungry. So I thought—why not try something simple? Just to test it."

He looked up at Oliver, his eyes glinting with something halfway between wonder and regret.

"I wished for a hamburger. Plain, with mustard. The kind I used to get at the fair." He let out a breath like it still surprised him. "And it appeared. Right there. On the shelf. Fresh. Hot. The smell hit me before I even saw it."

Oliver leaned in, stunned silent.

"I ate it right there in the pantry. Burned my tongue, I was so excited. And once it worked—once I knew—I couldn't stop. I asked for cherry pie next. Not just a slice—a whole pie. It came out warm, the crust still golden, juice bubbling through the cracks. Then mashed potatoes. Then a pitcher of lemonade. Then cinnamon rolls. I don't even know why—I wasn't even that hungry."

He shook his head slowly. "It just kept answering." His voice dropped, thickening with the weight of memory.

"The shelves filled up. Food piled onto the counters. Steam rose from dishes I never asked for—like the pantry had started giving on its own. Like it wanted to keep going."

His gaze darkened. "That's when the pastor came back. And caught me."

The room fell silent.

Oliver didn't speak. He barely breathed.

His grandfather looked down at his hands—weathered, still.

"I'll never forget his face. Not angry. Not confused. Just... disappointed. Like he already knew what was coming."

He sat back down, the weight of the moment settling across the room.

"So... that's why we were kicked out of the church?" Oliver asked gently.

"Not exactly," his grandfather replied. "But it started there."

He looked away.

"A week later, something terrible happened. My uncle and the pastor had a bitter argument. No one knows what it was about. And then... the pastor was dead."

His voice cracked slightly.

"My uncle didn't kill him, Oliver. But many believed he did. He was exiled. Became a pariah in this town. My father had to buy out his shares of the store, and my uncle left—moved to St. Louis to live with family."

He stared at the floor.

"After that... the church was closed. They said it was under investigation, but it never opened again."

Silence followed—cold and absolute.

After a long pause, Oliver's grandfather stood. He closed the grey ledger gently, then walked it back to the shelf and slid it between two other worn volumes.

With his back still to Oliver, he spoke again.

"When I inherited the company, I knew I had to buy the church and rectory. Not to exploit it... but to preserve it."

He turned halfway, his expression unreadable.

"Now that the Kravitz family has moved in, I've offered them a substantial sum for the home."

"Do you think the rock is still there?" Oliver asked quietly. "And... what would you do with the Giving Basket?"

His grandfather turned slowly.

An ear-to-ear grin spread across his face, his entire demeanor shifting—calculated, bright-eyed, electric.

"Well," he said, his voice brimming with excitement, "one day the store will be yours—after your father retires. But you, Oliver... you will be the one who truly reaps the rewards."

He leaned across the desk, eyes glowing.

"Think about it. We could create any meal, any food, with just a thought. We'd have a built-in restaurant. No food costs. No waste. The Henry Brothers Grocery could become world famous."

He stepped back, spreading his arms as if envisioning the empire.

"We'll make a fortune. The fortune my father and uncle always dreamed of."

Oliver swallowed hard, the pressure pressing against his chest like a stone.

Then his grandfather's voice dropped low, slippery and sharp.

"You said you're friends with their daughter?"

Oliver didn't answer—but his silence was enough.

"I need you to find a way to see the pantry for yourself," his grandfather said. "If they know what it is... they might not want to sell."

He smiled again, but this one didn't feel warm.

"It's a matter of Henry family destiny, Oliver."

"Do you think the rock is still there?" Oliver asked quietly. "And... what would you do with the Giving Basket?"

His grandfather turned slowly, and a broad, almost theatrical grin spread across his face. His entire demeanor shifted—no longer the quiet, reflective man recounting childhood memories, but someone energized, calculating, electric with purpose.

"Well," he said, his voice brimming with excitement, "one day the store will be yours—after your father retires, of course. But you, Oliver... you will be the one who truly reaps the rewards."

He stood up and moved around the desk, his steps quick and deliberate. His hands came alive as he spoke, painting pictures in the air.

"Think about it. We could create any meal, any food, with just a thought. Fresh produce. Gourmet meals. Seasonal favorites. Limited edition holiday specials—anything. We'd have a built-in kitchen, a miracle that never runs out. No suppliers. No spoilage. No overhead."

He leaned in, his eyes glowing with ambition.

"The Henry Brothers Grocery could become world famous. Imagine it—lines around the block. Orders flying in from across the country. A chain of stores. A legacy to rival empires."

He stepped back, spreading his arms wide as if presenting the kingdom already rising before him. "We'll make a fortune. The fortune my father and uncle always dreamed of. But this time, we won't let anyone stop us. No superstition. No secrecy. No pastors or pantry doors standing in our way."

Oliver sat frozen, his hands gripping the edge of the chair. A cold pressure settled on his chest. Not from fear exactly—but from something heavier. Like a stone, pressing down, reminding him that this moment mattered.

His grandfather's tone changed again, dropping low. Smoother. Sharper.

"You said you're friends with their daughter?"

Oliver flinched. He didn't answer—but his silence was enough.

"I need you to find a way to see the pantry for yourself," his grandfather continued. "If they know what it is... if they understand the value of what they've got, they might not want to sell."

He started pacing now, hands clasped behind his back.

"We'll have to be careful. Strategic. They'll think it's just an old house with a creaky door and a dusty pantry. But you and I—we know better."

He stopped and looked directly at Oliver again, his smile reappearing—but this one didn't feel warm. It didn't even feel human.

"It's a matter of Henry family destiny."

Oliver felt the words land like an avalanche. He looked down, his mind reeling. The boy who loved books and folklore was suddenly staring at a future written not in stories, but in deals and manipulation.

And for the first time, he wondered if he was being groomed not for a legacy—but for a lie.

Chapter 12

Can a Henry be Trusted?

The very next day, Pacing between the familiar history and philosophy sections of the school library, Oliver wore a faint track into the carpet beneath his feet. He muttered to himself, his mind racing, dragging each step like it bore the weight of a thousand unanswered questions.

He glanced at the clock. The minute hand inched closer to noon. The longest minute of his life finally gave way to the shrill cry of the school bell.

Pivoting sharply toward the library doors, Oliver fixed his eyes on the glass—just in time to see Eleanor sprinting toward him.

His heart leapt.

"Eleanor!" he whispered with urgency, motioning toward the back corner of the library. "C'mon, there's something we need to talk about."

Without waiting, he turned and scurried down the aisles, weaving through shelves toward their usual table near the dust-covered history books. Eleanor followed, sliding into the chair across from him. She dropped her notebook onto the tabletop with a soft thud.

She studied him carefully. Something was off.

"You're acting weirder than usual," she teased. "What's going on with you?"

Before Oliver could answer, she cut to the chase.

"What did your grandfather say yesterday?"

Oliver opened his mouth, then closed it. He hesitated.

"Well..." he started.

"Well, what?" Eleanor pressed, growing impatient.

Oliver exhaled. "You were right. My grandfather had a lot more to do with all this than I thought."

He paused. "But there's more."

Eleanor sat upright. Her eyes sharpened.

Oliver leaned forward slightly. "He wants to buy your house because... it's like a stain on our family name. The ban that stopped us from owning the church property? Now that your family lives there... your parents can lift it."

Eleanor's eyes widened.

"So it's true," she said, almost to herself.

"What is?"

"Your family was banished from the church!" she said, louder than she meant to.

Oliver winced. "Sort of? It's complicated."

He looked at her, unsure of how much more to say.

Eleanor narrowed her eyes and leaned in over the table, voice low and urgent.

"Go on, Oliver."

He scratched the back of his head, avoiding her eyes.

"My grandfather wants to buy the house to correct the past," he said slowly. "He wants to turn the church into a community restaurant."

"A restaurant?" Eleanor echoed, incredulous.

"Yeah... so the grocery store can be part of the experience. You know, giving back to the community—like... like the—"

He trailed off.

"Just like what?" Eleanor snapped. "Tell me!"

"Shhhh!" Oliver hushed her, finger to his lips. "Not so loud!"

He glanced around, then leaned in.

"I was going to say... just like the story of the Giving Basket."

"Oh really?" Eleanor asked, arms crossed. "Your grandfather wants to use the restaurant as the Giving Basket?"

"That's what he said," Oliver replied, fidgeting slightly.

"Oh, is that all he said?" she added, her smirk razor-sharp.

Oliver shifted uncomfortably in his chair, shoulders stiffening, his eyes darting toward the bookshelf. Beads of sweat formed at his brow as he tried to avoid Eleanor's gaze.

She noticed. And it only pushed her closer to the edge.

"Tell me. Now!" she demanded, raising her voice.

"Shhhh! Okay, okay—just keep your voice down! We're still in a library!" Oliver whispered, glancing around in panic. "He... he said the reason he wants to buy the church is because it's the original site of the Giving Basket legend."

Eleanor narrowed her eyes.

"My great-grandfather came here to find it," Oliver continued. "But by the time he arrived, the church had already been built over it. And now that it's no longer a functioning church... my family can legally purchase it."

Eleanor leaned forward, eyes locked on his. "You mean... your grandfather wants to use the Giving Basket for his own business?"

Oliver recoiled. "What are you talking about?"

"You heard me." Eleanor's voice sharpened. "He's not preserving anything. He's planning to profit off the magical pantry."

Oliver's body tensed, then slackened, snapping forward and back like a stretched rubber band.

"You really think your family can own something that was meant to help people?" Eleanor said, her voice full of heat. "Your family will never own the Giving Basket."

Oliver stared at her, stunned.

"I'm the protector of the stone now. And I will bring honor back to this town."

That landed like a thunderclap.

Oliver blinked. "What stone are you talking about?"

Eleanor's jaw tightened. "Don't play dumb with me."

"The Giving Basket," she snapped. "The stone your grandfather is trying to steal from under us."

Oliver sat frozen, the puzzle pieces scrambling behind his eyes.

"The magic... is real?" he asked, eyes wide with disbelief.

Eleanor leaned in with fire in her voice. "Oh, Mr. Mighty Historian, don't tell me you never learned about the real Giving Basket? Didn't your grandfather tell you all about it?"

She reached into her bag, pulled out her notebook, and slapped it onto the table—flipping to the sketch of the carved wooden staff.

"Here. Take a look for yourself."

Clearly spooked, Oliver sat bolt upright, eyes fixed on the notebook. He leaned in slowly, inch by inch, his expression shifting from alarm to awe as the image came into view.

His demeanor changed.

Gone was the anxious, fidgety boy from a few moments ago.

Instead—here was Oliver the researcher, the historian, the kid who lived to decipher mysteries like ancient scripts and artifacts lost to time.

"Where did you get this?" he asked, eyes locked on the drawing.

Without waiting for an answer, Oliver sprang up from his seat, darted around the table, and disappeared behind the bookshelf.

"Aha!" his voice rang from the next aisle.

Eleanor craned her neck to follow his movement.

Emerging from the Religions and Myths section, Oliver clutched a heavy book, already flipping through its pages with practiced hands.

He plopped back into his chair, eyes scanning rapidly—never once looking up.

Eleanor watched, surprised by how completely he had transformed. There was no trace of scheming, no hesitation—just pure focus.

In that moment, she saw it clearly.

This was the real Oliver.

"Right here, look!" he said, jabbing his finger at a page with excitement. "It matches your drawing."

Eleanor leaned over. "This looks exactly like my sketch," she said, flipping back to her notebook. "Same curves. Same symbols."

The two compared them—back and forth—searching for even the slightest difference.

"Eleanor," Oliver said, voice lower now, "I think this is your image. I think... this exact drawing comes from this book."

"What does it mean?" she asked, hesitating. The tone in her voice had changed—concern creeping in at the edges.

Oliver flipped to the next page. His eyes scanned rapidly, the text a blur—until one word stopped him cold.

He went still.

"Oliver?" Eleanor asked, picking up on the sudden shift. "What is it?"

He swallowed hard, voice dropping to a whisper. "Wendigo."

Eleanor blinked. "Wendigo? Isn't that some kind of... monster?"

Oliver didn't answer right away. He stared at the page as if trying to look through it.

"It's a symbol," he said finally, his tone tight. "A creature from Wamponoag legend. A spirit of hunger and greed. It brings famine... curses. It feeds on people, sometimes literally, sometimes through their choices."

He leaned closer to the drawing. "This sketch—this isn't just a warning. It's tied to the Giving Basket. Look," he said, pointing to a crude shape behind the beast. "That's corn. Or crops. Something with the farms."

Eleanor opened her notebook and flipped to a new page. "This is the other half of the image," she said, her voice rising with realization. "I thought it was symbolic... like a warning about using the magic selfishly. But now... I think it's more than that."

Oliver leaned over to look—and froze. His eyes widened as he took in her sketch. For a second, the world seemed to narrow to that single page. Then, with a sharp breath, he recoiled—his chair scraping loudly against the floor as he stumbled back.

A startled yelp escaped his throat.

Eleanor jumped.

He rushed forward suddenly, grabbing her by the shoulders. His hands were shaking. His eyes locked onto hers—wide, unblinking. He didn't speak. Just stared.

Then slowly, he let go.

His gaze dropped to the floor.

And finally, in a voice that was more breath than sound, he asked; "Is the Giving Basket stone... in your house?"

Eleanor hesitated.

The question didn't just hang in the air—it pressed into her. She could feel it echo in her chest, vibrating like a tuning fork against the core of everything she'd come to believe.

The weight of it.

The risk.

But also—the truth.

She looked at Oliver, saw the mixture of hope and fear in his eyes, and knew there was no more hiding.

"Yes," she said at last, her voice quiet but unwavering. She gave a single, steady nod.

In that moment, something passed between them—unspoken but deeply understood.

This was no longer just about strange pantry magic or missing historical records. It was no longer a school project or a half-remembered myth.

This was legacy. And responsibility.

A burden born not of choice, but of inheritance.

As above, so below.

Those ancient words, once cryptic, now felt carved into her very bones.

The silence returned—thicker than before. Sacred. Unshakable. They sat there, two kids on the edge of childhood and history, bearing the invisible weight of centuries in the making.

Neither of them moved. Neither of them spoke.

Eleanor felt the truth settle fully inside her, like the stone itself had rooted in her chest.

And then—softly—she broke the stillness.

"I'm the protector of the Giving Basket stone now," she said, her voice trembling with awe and certainty. She rose to her feet, the movement slow and intentional, like stepping into a larger version of herself. Her voice grew with every word, gaining strength, purpose.

"It's my duty to help this town. To guard what's been forgotten. To honor what was given, and never use it for greed."

She pressed her fist to her chest. "I swear it."

She took a breath, eyes focused—not on Oliver, but on something beyond him. Something larger.

"This town has lost a lot—memories, people, trust. But if the Giving Basket still exists, if the magic is still alive, then maybe... maybe we can bring something back. Not just food, or hope, but belonging."

She looked down, her voice softening.

"It doesn't matter that I'm just a kid. The stone chose my family for a reason. And I'm not going to let it down."

Then she looked at Oliver, her expression clear and firm.

"Someone has to protect it. Someone has to make sure it's used for good. And if that someone is me... then I'll do it with everything I've got."

Oliver sat for a long moment, hunched over, eyes locked on the floor. His thoughts swirled—his grandfather's voice, the old ship logs, the glowing stone, Eleanor's steady courage, and the quiet ache of knowing his family had stood on the wrong side of history more than once.

The gears kept turning.

Then—he stood.

He inhaled, long and slow.

And for the first time in his life, his voice didn't waver.

"Eleanor," he said, calm and sure, "I've spent my whole life digging through books. Tracing old names, forgotten places, stories no one believed mattered."

He looked her in the eye.

"But this... this matters. I thought I wanted the truth for me—for the Henry name. But now I see that this isn't about redemption. It's about responsibility. It's about preserving something sacred. Protecting something that could change everything."

He stepped forward, his posture firm, his eyes shining.

"I don't want to just study history anymore. I want to shape it. I want to be one of the good guys—the ones who stood up when it counted."

He grinned, heart pounding in his chest.

"So if you'll have me... I'm with you. All the way."

A beat passed. Then, with a spark of mischief returning to his eyes, he struck a pose, chin high and fists at his hips. "Oliver's my name..." he declared, loud and proud, "...and history is my game."

Eleanor laughed—a real, full laugh, the kind that lightens everything. She nodded, eyes shining. "Welcome to the team, Oliver. Let's protect the stone. Together."

Chapter 13

Cherry Pie with a Twist

The rest of the day slipped by in a blur for Eleanor. She couldn't focus. Not on math. Not on vocabulary. Not even on lunch. Her thoughts kept drifting back to the pantry—spinning through ideas like a carousel of magic. What else could she summon? What foods would Oliver want to try? Could they ask for something no one had ever tasted before?

She filled the margins of her notebook with doodles of pies, pasta, floating sandwiches, and steaming bowls of stew. At one point, her teacher called her name twice before she even noticed.

By the time the final bell rang, Eleanor was practically vibrating with excitement.

She grabbed her backpack and bolted out the classroom door, heart pounding with purpose. Today was the day. She was going to show Oliver the truth—the magic. Really show him.

But as she skidded to a stop at the edge of the bus line, scanning the familiar crowd of students, her excitement flickered.

No sign of Oliver.

She stood on tiptoe, craning her neck. Checked the usual spots. The bench. The tree near the bike rack. The edge of the sidewalk.

Nothing.

A knot of worry began to form in her stomach—until—

"Eleanor!"

She turned at the sound of her name cutting across the parking lot, sharp and clear.

There, just beyond the buses, standing near the street lamp with his clipboard tucked under one arm, was Oliver—grinning like he already knew she was coming.

"Eleanor!" Oliver yelled, waving her to come over.

Oliver's grandfather pulled up to the front of the school in a gleaming black car—windows tinted, grill polished, and engine purring like a show-off. Eleanor narrowed her eyes from the top of the school steps, clutching her backpack strap like a seatbelt.

"That's... not normal," she muttered.

Oliver didn't answer. He just blinked at the car like it had grown horns.

"Does he usually—?"

"Nope," Oliver cut in. "Not once. Not ever."

The passenger window glided down as if summoned by magic. Mr. Henry leaned toward the open space, sunglasses perched like a movie villain, smile fixed too tightly in place.

"There you are! I figured I'd swing by and give you two a lift. I'm already heading to the house, and I hear I'm expected for dinner. Isn't that right, Eleanor?"

Eleanor's stomach dropped like a basement elevator. She forced a smile, eyes flicking to Oliver.

"Right," she said slowly. "My parents invited you... Since you wanted to see the house."

"And talk," Mr. Henry added, smile stretching thinner. "About possibilities."

Eleanor didn't like the way he said that word. Possibilities. Like it came with terms and conditions. The same feeling you get from the slimy salespeople on infomercials.

Oliver gave the weakest shrug in the history of shrugging and muttered, "He must've talked to my mom. Or your mom. Someone's mom."

They rode in silence for a few minutes, save for the soft hum of the engine and the occasional glint of Mr. Henry's sunglasses catching the sunlight like a signal flare. Eleanor sat stiffly in the backseat, eyes bouncing between the window and the rearview mirror.

"So," Mr. Henry said casually, eyes still on the road, "how are you liking the old place, Eleanor? Cozy little church home. Bet there's a story in every wall."

"It's... historic," she replied.

"A real gem," he said with a smirk. "Of course, like most gems around here, it needs a little polishing. I imagine it's quite an adjustment after the city. Not exactly the fast lane out here."

"It's fine," she said flatly, resisting the urge to say; It's not yours.

Oliver fidgeted beside her. Mr. Henry continued, smooth as ever. "Your parents must be happy, though—good hours, stable work. Not many towns like this left with opportunities. I like to think we're doing something good for the community."

Eleanor said nothing.

"Of course," he added, "a place like that... needs a lot of work, but I think it's a little magical." Mr. Henry said with a grin while staring at Eleanor in the rearview mirror, attempting to read her facial expressions.

Eleanor, playing it cool so as not to tip her hand, replies with a melancholy, "I guess?"

The remainder of the ride continued in silence until reaching the front of Eleanor's house. She looked at Oliver with her eyes wide open to signify a silent plea about what was happening right now.

The black car pulled to a slow, deliberate stop in front of the house. The gravel crunched under the tires like it didn't want to give him a place to park. Mr. Henry stepped out first, adjusting his blazer like he was about to walk into a boardroom, not a peeling old rectory with crooked shutters and a front step that leaned to one side.

Eleanor climbed out next, catching Oliver's eye again and raising her eyebrows like are you seeing this too? Oliver responded with a shrug that said every second of it.

Charlie met them at the porch with a bark, trotting up the walkway with his usual bounce—until he caught sight of Mr. Henry. The dog froze, head low, ears back. A low, rumbling growl crept up from his throat like a warning siren set to low volume.

Mr. Henry paused mid-step. "Well hello, pup," he said with forced cheer, hands tucked politely behind his back. "What a handsome guard dog."

Charlie didn't wag his tail. He didn't move. Just growled and stared like he was looking at something Eleanor couldn't see.

"Charlie!" Eleanor's dad called from the doorway, already holding a dog treat, as to persuade Charlie from biting their guest. "Come on now, that's no way to greet a guest!"

He gave Mr. Henry a polite smile—one of those you-sign-my-paychecks kind of smiles—and bent down to grab Charlie by the collar. "Sorry about that, sir. He's usually much friendlier."

"No offense taken," Mr. Henry said. "Dogs are excellent for warding off intruders, I just met the fellow, he will learn to like me; people always learn to like me." He finished with a grin.

Charlie let out one short, snappy bark at that comment before being led inside and down the hallway to the kitchen.

"Pleasure's mine," he replied with a perfect grin, his eyes scanning the porch, the windows, the corners of the house as if memorizing the structure. "What a charming place you've got here. I was just telling Eleanor how special this house feels. Very... grounded."

He let the word hang for a beat longer than necessary, his gaze lingering on the floorboards beneath their feet.

Eleanor stiffened.

Her mom laughed lightly, brushing a strand of hair behind her ear. "Well, it's certainly old enough to feel grounded. I think it groans louder than we do after a long day."

Her dad stepped in, wiping his hands on his jeans. "Yeah, half the floor's uneven. We'll get around to fixing it—eventually."

Mr. Henry chuckled, but his eyes never stopped moving. "Sometimes the oldest homes have the deepest roots," he said casually. "You never know what's buried underneath."

Eleanor's dad raised a brow. "I hope it's not more plumbing issues. We've already found three leaky pipes."

Mr. Henry smiled again—tight, deliberate. "Ah, I was thinking more along the lines of... history. Foundations. The kind of things people overlook."

There was a brief silence.

Eleanor's mom glanced at her husband with a puzzled smile, then turned back to Mr. Henry. "Well, we haven't found any buried treasure yet, if that's what you mean."

"Not yet," Mr. Henry echoed, with a faint twinkle that didn't quite reach his eyes.

Eleanor folded her arms and stared at the porch railing, her jaw tight.

He didn't think they knew.

Not really.

And they were doing a great job of proving him right.

"Well," her father said with a clap of his hands, "dinner's not quite ready, but you're welcome to make yourself comfortable in the living room. We've got some drinks on the cart—and our daughter's promised us something spectacular."

"She's quite the cook," her mother added proudly. "Even our dog thinks so."

Mr. Henry chuckled. "Well then, I can't wait to see what magic she whips up."

Eleanor exchanged a quick glance with Oliver, and then both kids slipped past the adults toward the kitchen. They didn't need a reminder. They had work to do.

The moment they stepped into the kitchen, Eleanor let out a sharp breath she hadn't realized she was holding. "I think Charlie likes him less than I do," she muttered, grabbing a clean dish towel to dry her hands. The pantry door was already cracked open, almost like it had been waiting for her.

Oliver hovered near the counter, fiddling with his phone, eyes still wide. "That was weird. Even for him."

"You think?" Eleanor snapped, then softened her tone. "Sorry. I'm just... tense. He's too smooth. Like, 'I'm-hiding-something-under-my-smile' smooth."

Before either of them could say more, footsteps creaked in the hallway. Mr. Henry wandered toward the kitchen, his polished shoes pausing just short of the doorway. But before he could step in, Charlie appeared—silent and steady—planting himself firmly in the threshold like a furry sentry. The dog didn't growl, didn't bark, just stood there, head slightly lowered, eyes locked onto Mr. Henry with unnerving calm.

Mr. Henry hesitated, then took a slow step back, hands raised in mock surrender. "I can take a hint," he said smoothly, glancing at Oliver. "Why don't you make some drinks—loosen things up a bit, huh?" His voice was light, but his smile was strained.

Oliver nodded, scrolling through something. "Well, if we're serving drinks, we might as well make it good."

Eleanor raised an eyebrow. "You're planning cocktails now?"

"Nope. Just found this thing on retro mocktails," Oliver said, flipping his phone around to show her a glowing picture of a fizzy drink with mint. "It's called a Lime Rickey. Think you can magic this up?"

"Read it slowly," Eleanor said, already standing in front of the pantry, hand on the door.

Oliver cleared his throat with mock drama. "Crushed ice, fresh lime juice, fizzy soda water, simple syrup... and a mint leaf for flair."

Eleanor closed her eyes and focused. She imagined the drink exactly as described, even down to the beads of condensation running down the glass. A soft pop! filled the air, and when she opened her eyes, the drink was waiting on the middle shelf, glowing faintly in the low pantry light.

Oliver blinked. "That's both amazing and mildly terrifying."

"Welcome to my kitchen," Eleanor said, handing him the glass.

Charlie padded into the room, sniffing the floor near the pantry before plopping down with a grunt, eyes locked on the doorway like he was still on guard duty.

Eleanor glanced at Oliver and lowered her voice. "We need to stay sharp. He's here for more than just dinner."

"You think he knows about the stone?" Oliver replied.

"No. But I think he knows something. Enough to want this house badly." Eleanor remarks.

Oliver nodded slowly, setting the drink down with care. "Then I guess we better make sure the pantry knows it too."

In the living room, Mr. Henry settled into the patched-up armchair with the confidence of someone who didn't mind the missing cushion—because he assumed he'd own the whole place soon anyway.

Eleanor's mother sat upright on the loveseat, hands folded neatly in her lap, while her father leaned against the doorframe with a glass of water and a polite half-smile—his default setting for corporate overlords and forced social visits alike.

"I really do appreciate the invite," Mr. Henry said, crossing one leg over the other. "This town... it may look quiet on the outside, but it has potential. It just needs the right touch. People with vision."

Eleanor's mother nodded, ever the host. "Well, it's certainly been an adjustment, but the neighborhood's quiet. And we're grateful for the work."

"Of course," Mr. Henry said with a gleam in his eye. "You two have been fantastic additions to our team. And honestly, that's part of why I'm so interested in this place. Not just for the church or the real estate—though there is quite a bit of interest there—but for what it represents." He let the word hang in the air a second too long, like he expected it to echo.

Eleanor's father raised an eyebrow. "Represents?"

Mr. Henry nodded, smiling like a man unveiling a secret. "Tradition. Community. And maybe... something special." He chuckled lightly, waving his hand as if to brush off his own words. "I'm not one to chase fairy tales, but the Giving Basket legend? It always fascinated me as a kid."

"Oh yes," Eleanor's mother said, trying to keep the tone casual. "That old story. I think Eleanor mentioned they covered it in school recently."

Mr. Henry grinned wider. "Did she now? Smart girl. And I'll admit—I've always wondered if there's something to it. Not literal magic, of course," he added with a laugh, "but meaning. Value. That kind of legacy sticks with a place."

Eleanor's father took a long sip of water before replying. "So this dinner tonight... you're not just here for pot roast and polite conversation."

"Well, I wouldn't say just," Mr. Henry replied, flashing his teeth. "But yes. I wanted to speak to you both about something serious. An offer. For the house."

Eleanor's mother straightened slightly. "We've only just gotten settled."

Mr. Henry nodded. "I know. But I'm prepared to make it worth your while. I see a future here—a new type of food service. Imagine a place where anyone can walk in and get exactly what they're craving. Something personalized, elevated. A Giving Basket for the modern customer." He leaned in, elbows on knees. "With your help, of course. Steady work, expanded roles, generous salaries. It's not just about buying a house. It's about investing in a vision."

From the kitchen, faint clinks and the soft thud of footsteps could be heard, followed by what might've been Charlie sneezing.

Eleanor's father crossed his arms. "That sounds like a big undertaking."

Mr. Henry tilted his head, eyes sharp but smiling. "Big reward too."

Back in the kitchen, Eleanor carried a stack of plates to the dining table while Oliver followed with forks and mismatched cloth napkins they'd pulled from a box labeled, "Kitchen"

Charlie lay near the pantry, one eye open, his tail occasionally thumping against the floor like a nervous drumbeat.

"They're still talking," Oliver said under his breath, peeking through the doorway just far enough to see the adults still perched in the living room.

"Good," Eleanor replied, setting the last plate with a soft clink. "Let's make this look like hospitality while we listen in."

Mr. Henry's voice carried just enough for them to catch his cadence, smooth and practiced. "It's not just the house, of course. It's the potential of what the space offers. We'd retrofit the church into a takeout experience that adapts to the customer—personalized meals, fresh-made, unforgettable."

"Sounds expensive," Eleanor's dad replied, somewhere between skeptical and amused.

"Oh, I've run the numbers. My connections, our infrastructure—it'll pay for itself. But more importantly, it's a symbol. A Giving Basket reborn, right here in Point Rock. And I'd like your help in making that dream a reality."

Eleanor's mom responded softly. "You mean... you want us to stay and work for you again?"

"More than that," Mr. Henry said, and even from the dining room, they could hear the shift in tone—the drop into something more serious, more final. "I want to buy the house. The rectory. All of it. And I'm prepared to offer you two million dollars."

The room went quiet, even the floorboards seemed to hold their breath.

Eleanor froze in place, a stack of knives still in her hand. She looked at Oliver, who looked back at her with wide eyes.

"He thinks we're just going to sell it," she whispered.

"He thinks two million means he owns the pantry," Oliver murmured.

"He doesn't even know what he's buying," Eleanor said.

From the living room, Mr. Henry continued, "That's my offer. And I'll be honest—I don't like waiting. I'm prepared to make the paperwork happen tomorrow."

Charlie, still planted near the doorway, let out a low, rumbling growl.

Eleanor gave him a gentle pat. "Yeah. We heard it too."

Her mother's voice rose next, trying to smooth over the moment. "Why don't we move into the dining room? Dinner's just about ready."

Chairs scraped. Footsteps shifted. The murmur of adult conversation floated in—half-pleasant, half-tense—as the grown-ups made their way from the living room to the long table, silverware already set and flickering candles casting gentle shadows on the walls.

Eleanor slipped back into the kitchen, her face tight with frustration. She leaned against the counter, arms folded like armor across her chest. "He thinks this is some money-making magic," she muttered. "That he's going to franchise the pantry."

Oliver hovered near the fridge, still glancing over his shoulder like he expected Mr. Henry to walk in uninvited. "He talks like he's already bought it," he said quietly. "Like the stone's just another shelf item." Oliver hovered by the cart of clean dishes. "He's not wrong about one thing—it would make money. Too much money."

Eleanor shook her head, then glanced toward the pantry door. "We need to remind him that it's not his to take."

"Yeah," Eleanor said, eyes narrowing. "And it would ruin everything."

They both looked toward the pantry. Its door was still slightly ajar, the light inside pulsing softly, as if aware it was being discussed.

"So... what do we do?" Oliver asked, voice low.

Eleanor straightened. "We show him what the pantry does to people who treat it like a product."

Oliver blinked. "You want to test him?"

"I want the pantry to test him," she replied. "Let's see if it still knows the difference between a giver and a taker."

She opened the door to the pantry fully, the inside glowing faintly gold.

"Cherry pie," she whispered. "Let's start with that."

Oliver perked up. "He loves cherry pie. He told me once it reminded him of the first time he visited this place as a kid."

Eleanor nodded. "Then we'll give him what he wants. And see what he deserves."

One by one, she pulled pies from the pantry—each one perfect, fragrant, and warm to the touch. A soft stack formed on a rolling serving cart. Then another. And another.

Oliver helped add whipped cream, garnishes, and plates, his face somewhere between amusement and awe.

"We're going full dessert buffet?" he asked.

She turned to the pantry one last time. "Just... do what you do best," she whispered.

Charlie let out a soft huff behind them, his tail wagging once hoping for some pie as well.

The cart creaked gently as Eleanor rolled it into the dining room, the air suddenly filled with the warm, sugary scent of cherry pie. Golden crusts shimmered under the overhead light, each pie glistening with a glossy, deep red filling. Swirls of whipped cream crowned the tops, and just the faintest hint of vanilla and almond danced behind the tart cherry aroma.

Mr. Henry leaned back in his chair, smiling wide. "Well now," he said, his voice rich with delight. "Someone knows my favorite."

"I remembered," Oliver said simply, sitting down across from him.

Eleanor didn't say anything. She just parked the cart beside the table and started setting plates with quiet precision.

One by one, the family reached for a slice. Eleanor's dad took a forkful and let out a low, surprised "Mmm." Her mother nodded in agreement, eyes widening at the first bite. Oliver tried his and smiled—it really did taste like childhood summers and fairgrounds. Then Mr.

Henry took his fork, sliced off a corner, and lifted it to his mouth.

It was immediate.

His expression twisted before the bite even hit his tongue. A bitter, metallic stench seemed to rise off the plate—rotten cherries, sour vinegar, spoiled cream. He coughed once, then looked down in confusion. His fork hovered in midair, a thick glob of dark red sludge clinging to it like congealed blood. He blinked. The whipped cream had collapsed into a milky yellow foam, oozing across the crust like slime. Tiny black specks moved—legs—and then the unmistakable wriggle of a maggot revealed itself, nestled between the cracks of what had once been buttery golden flake.

Mr. Henry lurched back in his chair, mouth clamped shut, fork clattering to the floor.

"What in the—"

The stench grew sharper, as if something had died and been slow-roasted in a pie shell. Eleanor watched, arms folded.

"Is something wrong?" she asked.

Mr. Henry gagged, grabbing a napkin and spitting into it, his face flushing bright red. He snatched the plate and shoved it away, but a second later, he reached for another slice on impulse—frustrated, greedy.

That one was worse.

This time the cherries were grey. Flies buzzed out as the crust cracked open. The smell made the entire table stiffen, even Oliver's eyes went wide.

Charlie barked once from the kitchen.

Eleanor said it plainly in a low whisper that only her parents could hear. "The Stone knows."

Mr. Henry stood, breathing hard, lips curled in revulsion.

"I—this is a joke," he said, looking around the table like someone had swapped the food as a prank. "You're trying to embarrass me. What is this?"

Her mother's slice remained perfect. Her father had gone for seconds. Oliver's was clean.

Only Mr. Henry's pies had turned.

He stared down at them in disbelief, as if the food itself had betrayed him.

Mr. Henry grabbed another slice with shaking hands and stabbed into it with his fork. The pie split open with a sickening squelch. Rotten cherries. A swarm of flies. Mottled crust like dead skin.

He recoiled, growling under his breath, then reached for another. And another. Each one, the same.

Maggots. Mold. Rancid filling that oozed across the plates like it was alive and angry.

"Impossible," he spat. "They can't all be—"

He stood and leaned over the cart, stabbing into pies like a man possessed, like he could force one of them—just one—to obey him. The room filled with the sound of crust cracking and utensils clanging against ceramic.

His fork hit the edge of one final pie—the only one untouched, sitting pristine in front of Eleanor's father. Golden, glistening, a perfect swirl of cream and cherry.

"Go on," Mr. Henry said, voice cracking. "Try that one."

Eleanor's father paused. He looked at the pie, then at his daughter.

Eleanor gave the faintest nod.

He reached out and sliced into the pie with his fork. The inside was immaculate—cherries glistening, steam rising, crust still flaking.

Mr. Henry's breath caught in his throat. He reached across the table before anyone could stop him and yanked the plate toward himself.

The moment his fingers touched the edge of the plate, the transformation began.

Cracks spiderwebbed across the crust. The whipped cream liquefied, turning gray at the edges. The pie shuddered, as if something inside had come to life, and then began to collapse in on itself, molding and sinking into a foul, deflated mess. The air thickened with the sour stench of rot.

Everyone at the table watched in silence. No one moved.

Mr. Henry slowly backed away from the table, his face pale, lips parted.

Eleanor's father set his fork down and gently placed his napkin on the table next to the finished plates of pies.

Her mother stood quietly and began gathering the used plates.

There were no words exchanged—just a silent understanding. The evening was over. The test was complete.

Mr. Henry's hand trembled as he smoothed his jacket, his breath shallow. Then, without warning, he slammed his fist on the table. The force sent one of the forks skittering off a plate, clattering to the floor.

"This is absurd!" he bellowed. "This house is falling apart! It's a wreck! Mold in the walls, sagging floors, cursed pie carts! You're all sitting in a rotten, dilapidated, haunted husk and pretending it's worth something! I'm offering you a miracle! Two million dollars for this filthy dump and your patchwork furniture!"

He turned sharply, storming toward the door with long strides. "One final offer," he snapped. "Two million. You've got until tomorrow."

And with that, he flung the front door open with the night air poured in, replacing the foul-smelling stench from the rotten pies.

Mr. Henry stormed down the front steps, shoes crunching against the gravel as he made a beeline for his car. The sleek black paint reflected the porch light like oil on water, and he yanked the driver's door open with more force than necessary.

Behind him, Eleanor's parents stepped out onto the porch, calm but firm. "We're not interested," her father said, voice steady.

Mr. Henry paused mid-step, slowly turning to face them. "I'm sorry?" he asked, though his tone made it clear he wasn't.

"We won't be selling," Eleanor's mother added. "Not now. Not ever."

The air between them was cold and razor-thin.

Mr. Henry's eyes narrowed. "You realize what you're turning down? What you're risking? A deal like this—no one else would offer it."

"We're not 'everyone else,'" her father replied. "And this isn't just a house."

Mr. Henry looked past them toward the open front door where Eleanor stood, fists clenched at her sides, eyes shimmering with the effort not to cry.

He scoffed. "You'll regret this." Then, with a cruel smile; "Consider this your last day of employment. Both of you."

He turned sharply, coat flaring with the motion, and climbed into the car. The door slammed shut with a violence that echoed off the dead trees lining the driveway—sharp, final, like a gunshot.

The silence that followed was deafening.

Neither of Eleanor's parents flinched. They didn't even look at the car. Instead, they turned to their daughter.

Her mother stepped forward and crossed the porch slowly, carefully, like approaching someone made of glass. She placed a gentle hand on Eleanor's shoulder, her thumb brushing the fabric of her shirt in a small, soothing motion. Her father stood behind them, his expression quiet but resolute, offering her a firm, steady nod. It was an unspoken message that wrapped around her like a blanket; You did the right thing. We're with you. We're proud.

Eleanor didn't speak. She couldn't. Her chest ached with pressure—like a dam holding back a thousand things she wasn't ready to feel. A tear slipped from the corner of her eye. She turned her head just slightly, letting her hair fall across her face so no one would see.

From the driveway, the car engine hummed impatiently. Then the passenger window rolled down with a mechanical whine.

"Oliver," Mr. Henry barked, voice sharp and barking. "Get in. Now."

Oliver stood frozen at the edge of the porch, backpack slung over one shoulder, hands clenched around the strap. His eyes flicked between the car and Eleanor—between legacy and loyalty.

A moment passed.

And then, without looking at his grandfather, he turned to Eleanor with a calm so casual it almost felt like a joke.

"Hey," he said, voice light. "Mind if I borrow your bike?"

Eleanor blinked. "What?"

"Gotta burn off those calories." He gave her a crooked, boyish smile. "I'll bring it back tomorrow."

She stared, mouth slightly open—but she didn't stop him.

Before Mr. Henry could shout again, Oliver jogged around the side of the house, unlatched the gate, and wheeled the bike down the gravel path. In one smooth motion, he swung onto the seat and took off, pedaling hard into the night. The red reflector on the back blinked in rhythm with her heartbeat, growing smaller and smaller until it disappeared around the bend.

Mr. Henry leaned forward in the car, lips parted to yell—but then stopped. Something in his expression twisted. Anger, confusion... maybe even fear. Without another word, the window rolled up again, cutting him off like a curtain falling at the end of a failed performance.

The car backed out of the driveway slowly. Then, with a loud rev, it disappeared down the road.

Eleanor wiped her cheek with the back of her hand and whispered—just loud enough for the wind to carry, "The pantry knows."

And somehow, in the stillness that followed, it felt like the house was listening.

Chapter 14

The Call

The morning after Mr. Henry came over, the house felt a bit different.

The morning after Mr. Henry came over, the house felt different.

Not shaken. Not broken. Just... changed.

Eleanor lay in bed longer than usual, her comforter pulled up to her chest, eyes fixed on the ceiling as soft, muted light filtered through the slats of her window blinds. The air didn't feel heavy, like it had the morning after her nightmare. It wasn't tense or warning her of something coming. It was still. Quiet. Like the house itself was breathing slow for the first time in days.

Her dream had been different, too.

No falling. No chasing. No cryptic whispers or shadows in the pantry.

Just light.

She had been in a sunlit field, wildflowers swaying gently, and a distant sound of laughter drifting on the breeze. She couldn't remember who was laughing—maybe no one at all—but it felt safe. Like something had been watching over her. Guiding her.

She hadn't wanted to wake up.

But now that she had, the feeling remained—calm, warm, wrapped around her like a soft blanket still clinging to her shoulders.

Downstairs, she heard the quiet clink of ceramic mugs and the familiar sputter of the old coffee pot trying to do its job. More importantly, she heard voices. Her parents.

Not sharp. Not panicked. Not whispering like they were trying to hide something.

Just talking.

Real talking.

Eleanor sat up slowly, rubbing the sleep from her eyes and tilting her head to listen better.

Whatever today held, it was already starting on a better note.

In the kitchen, her mom leaned against the counter, hands wrapped around a chipped ceramic mug. "I mean," she was saying, "we've got a bit in savings. It's not ideal, but maybe it's time to try something new."

Her dad poured coffee into his mug and gave a tired half-smile. "We always said we wanted to do something for ourselves. Could be, now's the time?"

Eleanor waddled into the room, hair still a mess, sleeves too long. Charlie looked up from his place by the pantry door, tail thumping gently against the floor. He didn't bark. He just watched her. Waiting.

Eleanor flopped into the chair at the table. Her mom turned to greet her with a soft smile.

"How'd you sleep?"

"Like a brick," Eleanor mumbled, then added, "except the brick had weird dreams."

Her dad chuckled. "Welcome to adulthood."

There was a moment of silence before her mom added, with a glimmer of dry humor, "Well... at least we've got a magic pantry and don't have to worry about food."

Eleanor gave a weak smile and glanced at Charlie, who hadn't moved from his spot.

He was staring at the pantry now, ears perked.

Eleanor frowned. "Is it just me, or is he... waiting for something?"

The room fell quiet again. Not eerie. Just... expectant. Like the house.

Eleanor stood in front of the pantry, one hand on the frame. She wasn't even that hungry, just... curious. Like she needed to check in with it.

"I could go for toast," she muttered. "Or something sweet."

She opened the door.

Nothing happened.

No fresh scent. No glow. No quiet pop of appearance.

Just shelves. Empty. Still.

Charlie let out a quiet whine and rose to his feet, stepping forward like he, too, was confused. Then, the floor beneath them shifted—not much, just enough for Eleanor to feel a low vibration, humming up through her socks.

She gasped and stepped back.

The wood around the pantry creaked—not from age, but from intention.

The vibration grew stronger, more focused, zeroing in on a single point; the hairline crack in the floor where her father had once stood, hammer in hand, claiming, "The stone asked me to do it."

Eleanor knelt down slowly and placed her hand over the crack.

A pulse. Faint but steady. Ba-dum. Like a heartbeat. But not hers. It was alive.

Then, a second later, a low hum filled the room. It came from beneath the floorboards—not mechanical, not electrical. It was ancient. Deep. The kind of sound you feel in your chest more than in your ears.

Eleanor's eyes widened. Images began to form in her mind—not words, but impressions. The church commons. Tables are lined with food. Children laughing. Hands exchanging plates. Baskets overflowing.

It wasn't a memory. It was a message.

She whispered, barely audible; "You want a festival."

The moment she said it aloud, the pantry pulsed with light—a bright flash behind the shelves—and a piece of toast appeared neatly in her palm, warm and slathered in apple jam.

Footsteps thundered into the room. Her parents rushed in, breath caught mid-panic.

"Eleanor?" her mom called. "What's going on?"

Eleanor stood up slowly, eyes wide, voice calm but clear.

"We have to get the whole town together," she said. "The Giving Basket wants a festival."

The stone's message echoed through her long after the glow had faded. It wasn't just a request. It was an invitation. A promise. A purpose.

And Eleanor had heard it—deep in her bones. Something inside her had settled. The fear, the doubt, the questions—they had been replaced by something steadier. Something certain.

* * *

By lunch, Eleanor was practically buzzing—an electric current of purpose thrumming just beneath her skin. This wasn't nerves. It wasn't anxiety. It was clarity. She hadn't stopped thinking about the vision, the glow, the hum in the floorboards, or the way her father's toast had felt like more than coincidence.

The Giving Basket wasn't just asking.

It was summoning.

And she was done waiting.

She spotted Oliver tucked away at the back of the school library, buried in a thick history book, a bag of pretzels resting at his elbow. He was mid-chew when he looked up—and froze.

One glance at her face, and he snapped the book shut.

"What happened?" he asked, already on his feet.

Eleanor didn't answer right away. She just smiled—wide, determined, unstoppable.

"It's time," she said.

"Okay?" he questioned, "what is it time for, exactly?"

Eleanor slid into the seat across from him. "The stone spoke to me."

Oliver blinked. "Okay. New high score on the weird-o-meter. Go on."

She recounted everything—waking up, the silence, the hum, the vision, and the final pulse that delivered the toast into her hand like an offering. She kept her voice low, half-worried the librarian might materialize between the bookshelves.

By the time she finished, Oliver was staring, eyes wide, a pretzel frozen halfway to his mouth. "So... what do we do?" he asked, voice barely above a whisper.

"We hold the festival," Eleanor said, without hesitation. The words dropped like an anchor. Certain. Grounded. Unshakable.

Oliver sat back, chewing on the thought—then nodded, slowly at first, then with growing confidence. "We bring it back. Just like the stone showed you."

He yanked a piece of loose-leaf paper from his binder and immediately started sketching a flyer with bold strokes. "Giving Basket Festival—Saturday at noon... church commons... food, fun, music?"

Eleanor smiled. "Perfect."

He glanced up, the marker hovering over the paper. "But what about my grandfather?"

Her smile dipped just slightly—but only for a second. Then her jaw set. "He doesn't matter right now."

Oliver hesitated, searching her face. "You're sure?"

"I'm sure," she said firmly, eyes locked on his. "This isn't about control or secrets or who ends up on the front page. No one has to know about the pantry or the stone. But the town needs this. We *need* this."

She tapped the paper with her finger, her touch deliberate. "We're bringing it back."

Oliver grinned wide. "Old Point Rock tradition—reborn."

They bumped fists, the sound small but satisfying. Somewhere down the hall, the bell rang—loud, echoing through the corridors. But to them, it didn't sound like just another school period. It sounded like the first chime of a revolution.

* * *

By the time Eleanor and Oliver returned from school, the air around the rectory felt charged—brighter, looser, alive with purpose.

Something had shifted.

Eleanor's mom was already in motion, sleeves rolled up, hair tied back, moving with a kind of quiet determination. The church's front room had been almost completely cleared; boxes pushed neatly to one side, old pews stacked like puzzle pieces near the far wall. The creaky floorboards were swept clean, and the windows had been cracked open, letting in warm afternoon light and the faint scent of earth and dust.

Folding tables had been hauled in from the storage shed and lined up in two neat rows outside on the common shaded area. On top sat glass jars and chipped vases filled with whatever wildflowers could be scavenged from the gravel lot—dandelions, black-eyed Susans, goldenrod, and sprigs of something lavender-ish, maybe mint. They weren't perfect. But they were beautiful.

It wasn't polished or planned.

But it was real.

And it was happening.

"I figured," her mom said with a wink, "if we're hosting a miracle, we should at least tidy up."

Eleanor grinned and dropped her backpack at the door.

Out back, her dad was mowing what grass still grew in jagged patches between the weeds. He'd found the old trimmer in the basement, along with a rusted toolkit and a long-forgotten sign that read; "*In Memory of Pastor Holland.*" He propped the sign up near the church steps and got to work fixing the railing.

Charlie trotted between them all, supervising like he was the project manager.

Inside the house, Eleanor sat at the kitchen table with a yellowed recipe box. She flipped through index cards with her mother's handwriting and her grandmother's, too. Some had smudges. Others had tiny grease rings in the corners. All of them smelled faintly of cinnamon and time.

"What about cornbread muffins?" she asked.

Her mom nodded. "And jalapeno jam. Remember how much your grandma loved it?"

"I do now," Eleanor said with a smile.

By dusk, string lights had been strung between the trees near the commons. The pantry had provided everything they asked for—within reason—and Eleanor began to understand that it didn't just grant wishes.

It responded to intention. To heart. And something in it seemed to be rooting for them.

* * *

By the next morning, Oliver had already printed the first stack of flyers. They weren't fancy—just black and white on plain paper, printed at the library after convincing Mrs. Newman to give them a few extra credits on the school account.

The words were simple, but bold:

Giving Basket Festival
Saturday at Noon – Church Commons
Food · Music · Community
(All are welcome)

Eleanor and Oliver made their rounds after school, their backpacks stuffed with folded flyers and their fingers smudged with ink from hand-cut stamps. They moved with a mission, their footsteps light and quick, the rhythm of their work becoming almost musical.

They taped flyers to telephone poles wrapped in layers of old tape and rusty staples. They pinched them under windshield wipers. They slid them under doors and between gas pumps, tucked them into library books between pages marked with pressed flowers and forgotten receipts. At the market, they left a small stack on the counter next to the gum and paper mints, the cashier eyeing them curiously before giving a quiet thumbs-up.

At first, people chuckled. "Giving Basket? Like that old town story?" "Wasn't that some church thing from, like, the sixties?" "Thought it was just a campfire myth."

But by the third flyer, someone at the diner said, "Didn't your grandfather used to talk about that?" And by the sixth, someone else said, "That was always such a good time. They used to do pie contests, didn't they?"

Eleanor's heart fluttered each time a new connection sparked—like matches striking gently in the dark.

At school, the buzz started small. A whisper in the hallway. A glance in the cafeteria. Then a teacher asked for a flyer. Mrs. Newman posted one outside her classroom door with a sparkly pushpin and smiled knowingly when Eleanor walked past. In the library, the old librarian didn't say anything. She just nodded once, slipped a blank envelope across the counter, and inside were twenty clean flyers—already copied and trimmed. Eleanor was just about to say something, but the librarian had already gone back to stamping due dates.

Even Oliver's older cousin, a senior who usually pretended not to know him, nodded once from across the hallway and said, "Hey. I heard about your festival thing. Might check it out."

By Friday afternoon, it had reached a quiet hum—everywhere and nowhere all at once. Flyers fluttered in breezes like bright little flags of possibility. Whispers turned to conversations. Conversations turned to plans. Some students were going just to see what it was. Others were dragging their parents, their neighbors, their younger siblings. A few teachers mentioned they'd "stop by" with the kind of offhand tone that meant they'd already marked their calendars.

Even the old man who ran the mechanic shop gave Eleanor a slow nod when they posted one in his window. "The town could use something like this again," he murmured. "Something good for once, it's been too long."

Eleanor and Oliver exchanged a glance as they stepped back out into the street, the sky deepening into late afternoon gold.

And while no one said it directly, not in so many words, Eleanor could feel it settling into the air around her—warm, subtle, and impossible to ignore. Hope was catching.

And it was spreading. One flyer at a time.

* * *

That night, the house was quiet again, but this time it wasn't holding its breath. It was resting.

Eleanor slipped out the back door just after dusk, careful not to let the screen slam shut. The air was cool, still tinged with late summer warmth, and the stars had started to poke through the indigo sky above the church steeple. Charlie padded after her, silent except for the soft thump of his paws on the packed earth.

She carried a candle in a mason jar—one of the old ones from the cellar—and lit it with a match she struck against the stone steps. The tiny flame flickered, then settled into a steady glow as she placed it at the top of the church walkway.

The commons were quiet, too. Tables were set. Lanterns had been strung between tree branches and rafters. Folded chairs waited patiently, like the whole place had taken a deep breath and was ready to open its arms.

Eleanor sat down on the top step, pulled her knees to her chest, and watched the candle dance. Charlie settled beside her, head on his paws, eyes facing out over the commons.

She didn't say anything at first. She didn't need to. There was no hum tonight. No pulse. No vibration. Just presence.

She looked out toward the commons and whispered, "We're ready."

After a few long moments, she stood and made her way back inside, pausing once at the pantry. Without a word, she opened the door, It didn't glow. It didn't hum. It just sat there. Waiting.

Charlie lay down near the pantry, gave one soft huff, and closed his eyes.

Eleanor turned off the light. "They'll come," she whispered to the dark. "You already know they will."

Chapter 15

Keeper of the Secret

Eleanor woke up an hour later than usual, but for once, it wasn't because she'd overslept—it was because she'd finally rested. Deeply. Peacefully. The light coming through her window was warmer than before. Golden. She didn't know if it was magic or just the way the sun happened to hit the glass, but either way, it felt right.

She stretched, yawned, and then peeked out her bedroom window. Down below, her parents were already in motion, moving with quiet urgency. Like worker ants, they carved steady paths from the house to the nearby church commons. Blue and white party tents stood tall across the field like sails on anchored ships, fluttering in the soft breeze.

Her dad was placing out folding chairs, arranging them in neat rows. Her mom moved between tables with boxes of decorations—flowers, small centerpieces, bundles of twine-wrapped silverware. They weren't rushing. They were ready.

Eleanor dressed quickly and made her way downstairs, where the kitchen buzzed with the hum of preparation. Charlie sat beside the pantry, tail sweeping the floor in long, content arcs. He was alert, but not anxious, like he knew this day had been coming.

Her mom and dad pushed through the kitchen doors, arms full of streamers and tablecloths.

Her dad caught sight of Eleanor and grinned. "Hey kiddo, think you can make some breakfast from the magic pantry? Your mom and I have been nonstop since sunrise. We're working up a real hunger."

Eleanor nodded with a spark in her eye. "Of course! Eggs, bacon, hashbrowns, toast, and jam?"

Her mom interjected from behind a stack of floral garlands, "I like scrambled—your dad likes sunny side up!"

Eleanor laughed. "Noted."

She stepped up to the pantry, cracked her knuckles, and placed her hand on the frame. "Let's do this."

She pictured a memory—Chicago, the hotel's continental breakfast buffet, towering trays of options, and the smell of syrup and fresh bread. One by one, she pulled out trays: crisp bacon, sizzling sausage links, golden hashbrowns, and eggs in every style imaginable—scrambled, over easy, hard-boiled, and Benedict with a perfect hollandaise drizzle.

Next came fresh fruit, stacked like a rainbow; strawberries, pineapple, kiwi, and melon. Cereal boxes appeared in a neat stack, beside bowls of yogurt with swirls of honey on top. Toast and jam practically popped into her hands, and she was grinning ear to ear by the time she turned around.

After the last tray—one filled with warm danishes, jelly donuts, chocolate croissants, and lemon poppyseed muffins—Eleanor carried it to the table, took a donut, and popped it into her mouth.

"This was my favorite from Chicago," she said around a mouthful, puckering her lips with exaggerated delight.

Her parents stared at the spread with a mix of awe and mild panic.

"What?" Eleanor said with a playful shrug. "I'm just making sure I'm ready for the festival. I'm going to try my hardest to provide the best Giving Basket Festival ever!"

Charlie barked once, approvingly, and licked then ate a sausage that rolled off the tray onto the floor.

* * *

By midmorning, the commons had begun to buzz. It started with just a few familiar faces—neighbors who lived close enough to walk, or maybe just didn't want to admit they were curious. Then more families came. And then clusters. Eleanor could hardly believe how quickly the field filled.

The Johnsons were the first to say something nostalgic. "I remember this from when I was a kid," Mr. Johnson said, adjusting his ball cap." His wife nudged him playfully and added, "Glad someone's bringing it back."

The Ferro family stopped by one of the long tables to complement the floral decorations. "These are gorgeous," Mrs. Ferro told Eleanor's mom. "It feels like the old days."

And kids—kids from school that Eleanor only knew from hallway glances—started showing up in twos and threes. Some nodded when they saw her. A few smiled.

She smiled back. Maybe things really were changing.

A small group of local musicians had set up on the church steps, providing an impromptu bandstand. Guitars were tuning, someone was setting up a snare drum, and faint music floated through the air like a warm-up act for something bigger.

Back in the kitchen, tucked out of view from the crowd, Eleanor was assembling her team. Her parents. Oliver. And herself. The pantry door stood open behind them, its glow a soft amber. Charlie sat outside the kitchen door like a guard dog at a secret club.

Eleanor pulled them in tightly, shoulder to shoulder, and gestured for everyone to join hands. "Okay," she whispered. "Before we start... thank you. I know this is a lot. I know it's strange. But we're not just making food today—we're feeding something deeper. And the pantry... it knows."

They all nodded.

Eleanor placed her hand over her heart and bowed her head for a moment. No words. Just intention. Then she turned to the pantry. "Let's cook!"

The pantry responded instantly. With a warm, golden pulse, the first tray appeared: thick slices of rosemary focaccia, still steaming, infused with olive oil and sea salt. Eleanor handed it to her father without a word.

Next came a massive platter of chicken cacciatore—slow-braised in tomatoes and herbs, garnished with dark green olives and sprigs of thyme. Then a dish of ratatouille, layered like a rainbow mosaic, the vegetables glistening with garlic and butter.

Eleanor reached back in. Paella emerged—bursting with saffron rice, mussels, shrimp, and roasted peppers, all arranged in a wide copper dish that shimmered under the kitchen lights.

Oliver whistled. "That's Spain, Italy, and France in four dishes."

"Just wait," Eleanor grinned. She pulled a tray of Picanha—juicy Brazilian sirloin, seared with crispy fat caps, sliced thin and laid beside bowls of chimichurri. Then came roasted potatoes with rosemary, truffled mashed potatoes, sweet potato casserole, and even waffle fries stacked like a Jenga tower.

Her mom nearly dropped a platter. "Are those... scalloped potatoes with Gruyère?"

Eleanor winked. "You said go all out."

Next came the salad bar—towering bowls of crisp arugula, shaved fennel, heirloom tomatoes, toasted walnuts, and thick, creamy dressings in jars that chilled themselves on contact.

With every dish, the pantry's glow brightened. The kitchen filled with warmth—not just physical, but emotional. Eleanor felt it in her chest, like a rising tide of gratitude and purpose. But she wasn't done.

She flipped open her favorite section of the family cookbooks—the desserts—and placed her hand on the pantry door. "This one's for the finale."

The glow intensified.

Out came pistachio macarons, lemon tarts, tiramisu, custard in crystal cups, yogurt and fruit woven like stained glass. Then came pecan pie, Boston cream donuts, and churros dipped in chocolate ganache. But the crowd favorite—the one Eleanor knew would win them all—was the ice cream sundae bar that appeared like a dream; hand-scooped vanilla, strawberry, and chocolate with every imaginable topping—fudge, sprinkles, cherries, cookie crumbles, and whipped cream that never melted.

Tray after tray, Eleanor passed them into the hands of her parents and Oliver.

With each new round, the cheers from the commons grew louder. Lids popped. Laughter echoed. A hum of joy buzzed through the crowd like electricity on a summer night.

Somewhere in the crowd, someone shouted, "Who made this brisket?!"

Eleanor wiped her brow, the edge of her sleeve damp with effort and heat, and smiled.

They had no idea.

But the pantry did.

It started with the flowers. A bare patch of earth near the church commons—dry, compact, and lifeless just that morning—had erupted into bloom. Wildflowers burst from the ground as if coaxed by sunlight alone; cornflowers, daisies, sweet alyssum, bursts of blue, violet, and bright white that shimmered like spilled paint on canvas.

Mrs. Ferro, carrying a plate of macaroni and a mason jar of lemonade, slowed to a stop and blinked at the sight. "I swear that was just dirt an hour ago," she said, crouching to smell a fresh cluster of daisies. "I walked right over that spot!"

A few others joined her, murmuring in wonder.

Then came the breeze.

There had been no wind in the forecast. No clouds. Just the steady warmth of a spring afternoon.

But now a soft gust curled through the commons—gentle, fragrant, impossibly specific. It smelled like cinnamon and cherry pie. It wove through the crowd, lifting hats, tugging gently at sleeves, tousling hair. Heads turned. Eyes closed. A few people stopped mid-sentence just to breathe it in.

Someone laughed. Another clapped without knowing why.

And then the birds came.

At first, just a few—sparrows, robins, a cardinal or two. But within moments, more arrived, fluttering down like notes from an unseen songbook. They perched along the old church steeple, the power lines, even the tops of the tents. Dozens of them, still and watchful.

Then, as if responding to a cue only they could hear, they began to sing.

Not the usual discordant chirping, but something more... melodic. The rhythm was loose, but intentional. Their calls rose and fell in perfect intervals, weaving in and out like harmony lines.

Below them, the local band had just finished a folk tune. The drummer, still holding his sticks, looked up.

"...Did they just start in key?" he whispered.

"Count us back in!" someone hissed.

"One... two... three... four."

And just like that, the band picked up again—this time playing with the birds. The melody shifted slightly, adjusted, adapted. It didn't matter what song they were supposed to play next. They followed this one instead.

It was as if the birds were reading the sheet music right out of the wind.

A hush of awe settled over the crowd, not quiet but reverent. People didn't ask questions. They just listened.

Eleanor, watching from the edge of the commons, felt a weight she hadn't known she was carrying lift off her shoulders. This wasn't just a festival. It wasn't just a comeback story for a town nearly forgotten by time.

This was magic—real and unhidden.

And the town was singing with it.

And then someone said, "This table hasn't run out once. I swear. I've been watching it for twenty minutes." It was the donated food table. A few families had brought pies, some breads, a big thermos of lemonade. But no one had been refilling it. Not visibly. Yet the food kept coming. And not just refills—new things. Dishes that no one could quite place, or pronounce, but tasted like childhood and holidays and something worth remembering.

One man bit into a fluffy spiral pastry he'd never seen before. "What is this?" he mumbled through a mouthful.

His daughter shrugged. "No clue. But I got two more."

No one said the word magic. Not out loud. But people lingered longer. They smiled wider. They sat on picnic blankets, elbow to elbow, talking to neighbors they hadn't spoken to in years. Children ran barefoot between the tents. Old friends embraced near the buffet line.

And somewhere, Eleanor stood behind the kitchen door, watching it all unfold through a narrow crack. Her heart was full. The Giving Basket wasn't just being remembered. It was remembering them back.

The hum of the festival faltered for just a moment when the black car pulled into the lot.

It didn't screech or roar. It rolled in—slow, deliberate, glossy like ink against sunlight. It parked under the shade of the lone oak, and the door opened with a click that sounded louder than it should have. Mr. Henry stepped out in a dark gray suit, sunglasses still perched on his face. His posture was straight, chin slightly lifted. Not a smile in sight.

Every step he took left a mark—literally. The grass beneath his polished shoes flattened into yellowed patches, like the very earth recoiled from him. It was as if the magic of the festival knew. And it didn't want him there.

He moved like a guided missile, weaving through the clusters of guests, nodding only when nodded to. People stepped aside, not out of courtesy—but habit. Respect laced with unease. No one welcomed him.

He found Eleanor's parents at the buffet, arms full of fresh trays. "I see your business is booming," he said, his voice crisp but cold.

Her mom's smile didn't falter. "It's not business. It's the festival."

Mr. Henry reached into his pocket and pulled out a folded sheet of paper. "Still stands. One-point-five million. That's my final offer." His voice was louder than before. It cut across the chatter, quieting conversations around them. A ripple of silence spread through the tables.

Eleanor stepped forward, wiping her hands on her apron, face calm. "It's not for sale."

He turned toward her slowly, sunglasses reflecting her silhouette. "This is your future we're talking about, Eleanor."

"No," she replied. "It's yours that you're afraid of."

A murmur stirred through the crowd—soft at first, like wind rustling through tall grass.

Someone near the back broke the silence. "You've done enough, Henry. Let it be."

Another voice followed—sharper, louder. "You only ever showed up when there was a camera."

Heads turned. Shoulders squared. The energy shifted.

"My granddad lost his farm over one of your 'partnerships!'"

"I remember when you shut down the bakery—just to buy the land!"

"You're not the heart of this town anymore."

Voices rose—decades of silence cracking open all at once. It wasn't a riot, but it was a reckoning. Resentment long buried was finding daylight again, and it was loud, clear, and pointed directly at him.

Mr. Henry stood frozen in the center of the commons, surrounded but suddenly alone. His jaw clenched. His eyes narrowed. For a breathless moment, it looked like he might shout back—might try to reclaim control with force, with pride, with fury.

But then he saw it.

The food—shared freely, without price tags or power plays.

The flowers—sprouting from bare earth like a blessing.

The music—intertwined with birdsong and laughter.

The people—arms linked, voices raised, eyes shining not with fear, but hope.

He was outnumbered. Outclassed. Out of place.

And then—from the side of the crowd—Eleanor stepped forward.

She moved slowly, deliberately, balancing a wooden tray in her hands. Her posture was steady. Her eyes locked on Mr. Henry's, not with anger, but with something stronger; conviction.

The tray, lined with perfect, individual cherry pies—each one shining under a swirl of whipped cream, buttery crusts browned just right, steam rising gently in the sun.

She stepped closer and held the tray out to him, steady as stone. "Mr. Henry, this pie is for you."

He eyed it warily, suspicion tightening the corners of his mouth. His voice dropped low, just above a growl. "I'm not falling for that trick again."

Eleanor didn't flinch.

She glanced at the crowd. Dozens of people were already eating—savoring each bite of their cherry pies with soft hums of delight. Smiles. Closed eyes. Laughter. No one gagged. No one flinched. Just the quiet, collective sound of a town remembering what it felt like to come together.

She looked back at him, her voice calm but firm. "If you want to be part of this—really part of this—then this pie is your choice. Not as a buyer. Not as an owner. But as a neighbor."

She softened just slightly. "If you believe in that... this'll be the best pie you've ever had."

A beat of silence.

Every eye in the commons turned to him. The music had stopped again, even the birds had quieted—waiting.

Mr. Henry stood motionless.

Then, slowly, he reached out, fingers trembling just slightly as he took the plate from her hands.

He stared at the pie. Then at Eleanor. Then back again.

The moment stretched.

Time—just for a second—held its breath.

He stared at the slice for a long time.

The crowd held its breath.

The crust was golden, still warm to the touch, the filling glistening like stained glass in the afternoon light—deep red, rich and sticky, the aroma rising in a soft, familiar wave; cherries, cinnamon, and something older. Something home.

Mr. Henry's hand trembled slightly as he lifted the fork. He hesitated mid-air, eyes darting to the crowd, to Eleanor, to the slice—like some part of him still couldn't trust it.

Still couldn't trust her.

Still couldn't trust himself.

Then he took a breath—deep and shaking—and brought the bite to his mouth.

The second it touched his tongue, everything around him vanished.

The commons, the people, the weight of expectation—it all fell away like dust in the wind.

He closed his eyes.

And he was somewhere else.

The scent of yeast and spice. The creak of old wooden floorboards. The clatter of pans in a sunlit church kitchen. A boy—maybe nine, maybe ten—perched on a stool too tall for him, legs dangling. In his small hands, a warm slice of cherry pie, steam rising in soft ribbons. Sweet. Tart. Perfect.

Across the counter, a man's voice—his father's—low and kind; "This is the kind of magic you don't mess with, son. You protect it."

The memory hit him like a wave—undeniable and whole.

His chest tightened. Not with pain, but with something he hadn't felt in years.

Belonging.

When he opened his eyes again, they were glassy. His shoulders softened. The tight line of his jaw uncoiled. And for the first time in what felt like a lifetime, he looked small—not weak, but young again. Human.

He cleared his throat, blinked once, and turned to Eleanor, voice barely above a whisper.

"Thanks, dear." He set the empty plate gently back on the tray, his fingers lingering there for a beat too long. "This is the best cherry pie I've ever had."

He smiled—softly, honestly. "You did really good, kid."

And in that moment, the town didn't cheer. They didn't clap. They simply breathed again. Together.

Then, just as quickly as he had arrived, Mr. Henry turned on his heel and began walking toward his car. The crowd didn't stop him. No one needed to. The moment had done what words couldn't.

The grass bent beneath his careful steps, and as he passed, it slowly stood back up—like the land itself was beginning to forgive him.

But before he could reach the driver's door, a figure stepped into his path. The librarian. She stood tall, calm, her cardigan sleeves pushed to the elbows, a knowing look in her eyes. She said nothing. Just opened her arms.

There was a pause.

For a heartbeat, Mr. Henry looked like he might resist. Like pride would pull him back. But then, without a word, he stepped forward and accepted the embrace. Not stiffly—not out of politeness—but fully, like someone who had been waiting for a hug far longer than he realized.

After a moment, they pulled apart, and without needing to ask, they walked to the nearest bench beneath the shade of an old oak tree.

Together, they sat.

And in the quiet hum of the festival—amid music and laughter and the scent of sweet pies cooling in the breeze—they began to talk.

Not as enemies.

Not as ghosts of the past.

But as old friends, finally catching up.

* * *

As the sun dipped lower behind the church steeple, the commons glowed in amber light. Lanterns flickered. Picnic blankets were scattered like islands of laughter. The band played soft, easy melodies—more lullaby now than anthem.

Eleanor's father climbed the wooden steps of the church, still in his rolled-up sleeves and apron, and raised a glass of sparkling cider.

The crowd quieted.

"I'm not much of a speechmaker," he began, "but I do know this—today reminded me what it feels like to belong to a town that shows up. To help. To listen. To eat." Laughter rippled gently. "We've been through a lot. Some of us lost jobs, some lost hope, and some lost sight of what makes a place worth calling home. But today..." He glanced around the field, eyes misting. "Today we remembered."

He lifted his glass slightly higher. "To neighbors who show up without being asked. To pies that taste like memories. To music, and laughter, and food, and all the little things that make a town feel whole again."

"To giving," someone shouted from the crowd.

He smiled. "To giving. And to the Giving Basket."

The crowd erupted in cheers, glasses raised high, cider fizzing in the golden light.

Eleanor stepped up beside her father, taking the mic with both hands. "This festival is a gift," she said. "And we wanted to give it back to all of you."

She paused, scanning the crowd. "The Giving Basket legend is back."

A few people clapped. Then more. Then all. A standing ovation of picnic chairs and applause under the setting sun.

A hush followed.

Someone sniffled. A kid cheered. And then the music picked up again, ushering in the evening like an old friend coming to stay.

By the time dusk fully settled, the commons had softened into a sea of glowing lanterns and satisfied silence. Lawn chairs were half-empty now, their owners slowly drifting toward the exit paths with full bellies and full hearts. The last chords from the band faded into the night, and the food tables were finally, mercifully still.

Eleanor sat on her porch steps overlooking the common, apron stained, hair wind-tousled, arms folded in quiet pride. Her heart was full—but not in the loud, exciting way.

Full like a warm blanket. Full like peace.

Behind her, Charlie lay near the door of the kitchen, his nose twitching as he sniffed at the evening breeze. He hadn't moved much all day, quietly watching each tray that passed, tail thudding lightly whenever a child dropped a scrap or a friend passed by with a smile.

The back kitchen door creaked open. Just a crack. Left ajar. Maybe on purpose.

Charlie's ears perked. He stood, stretched, and trotted inside.

No one noticed.

Not even Eleanor—though maybe, somewhere deep inside, she knew.

Inside the kitchen, the pantry door was glowing faintly—still open just enough to cast a soft halo across the floorboards. The trays were gone, the magic calmed, but something shimmered on the lower shelf.

A platter of brisket. A full one.

Charlie sniffed once, let out a delighted howl and gruff, and nudged the door the rest of the way open with his nose.

Then, with one joyful huff, he pulled the tray down and began to feast—tail wagging like a flag in a summer breeze, paws crossed like he'd done this before. When he was done, he curled up right in front of the pantry, nose tucked under one paw, belly full and spirit satisfied.

The pantry dimmed to a gentle glow, and the house once again felt still—not because it was waiting...

...but because it was content.